DEZI GOLDEN

My hero
My Love

---

1.   http://www.dezigolden.com

To those who understand that a true hero is measured not by strength but by the heart...

Chapter 1

Great Dane

"I wanted to welcome you to Melbye. It's a thing."

H

azel thanks the bartender for bringing her another beer and watches her walk passed the group of twenty-something girls two booths away. They seem harmless. She can tell they're a sorority from their common look and close-knit sharing of a pitcher of light draft. It brings back memories she's not needing to reminisce. A gentleman in a chef's shirt comes through the kitchen door carrying her meal. She smiles at the thought that how no matter who you are, when you bring food to the table, others are always happy to see you.

Tommy, as his name tag reads, smiles brightly and places her plate down. "Is there anything else I can get you?"

"Would you have any Crystal hot sauce by chance?"

He winces, "We do not but, would Tabasco do?"

"It will, thank you."

He pivots and walks towards the bar waving to the girls in the booth. They reciprocate, one blowing fake kisses at him. He pretends to stumble as he catches an invisible kiss to the cheek. Hazel finds it all rather humorous and enjoys the energy that seems to abound in the tiny bar and grill. Tommy ducks under the bar slab and reaches for the hot sauce showing the bartender the small jar and she nods. He rushes back towards Hazel.

"Here you go."

"Thank you so much uh, Tommy?" Hazel squints to read his name.

"No problem. Trudy will be by to check on you." He points towards the bartender and rushes off.

Hazel's mouth waters, she can't remember the last time she had a BLT with french fries and a beer. It's not the healthiest meal, but befitting for her new life in a new town.

The pleasant background music of the dark bar is interrupted by a barrage of commotion and noise through the front door. Trudy, behind the bar, reaches up and pulls a short rope connected to a large brass bell above her cash register, ringing it loudly for the eleven or so firemen entering. The patrons in the bar, along with the sorority group, all begin hooting and clapping. Some even give a standing ovation. The firemen begin to bow and nod in appreciation, most of them sweaty and dirty. They're smiling and are jovial towards each other. The smell of smoke wafts across the room. Hazel chews, thinking some sort of fire incident went as planned. She likes how close and affectionate the crew is with each other.

She takes another bite of her sandwich, elbows resting on the table and chews watching their celebration. She's not so sure about the town of Melbye yet, but so far it seems to reflect camaraderie, at least amongst the locals. She's been wondering why Grandma Elsie insisted on her moving here for "no less than six months" while finding a Mr. Merrill Clement and interviewing him for her next novel.

MY HERO MY LOVE

Just as the noise settles and the murmur of conversation takes over, the crowd begins to push out chairs and barstools as most find their feet and clap in another standing ovation. This one, is way more intense with loud whistling and yelling. Hazel stops chewing and turns to where they're all looking. The door had opened again, a tall white-haired man enters and steps to the side. Behind him in almost slow-motion an even taller, adonis of a man resembling him steps in and smiles humbly. He waves shyly and Trudy rings the bell again. The sorority girls begin shouting "Great Dane, Great Dane, Great Dane!" in unison, causing the whole bar to follow. Hazel sees him wave at them and try to quiet everyone. His hair is tousled and he has a cut along his cheek but otherwise he's about as good looking as Tom Sellek and Scott Eastwood in one package. Hazel huffs and turns back to her food thinking how it should be illegal for a human to be so attractive.

Dane blushingly begins to shake hands and receive pats on the back. His father pulls out a bar stool for him in the middle of the crew and one of them hands Dane a mug. He's smiling from ear to ear, yet obviously uncomfortable with all the hype. He obliges and sits down in a direct line of sight across the bar from Hazel's table. He laughs with the others but notices her sitting alone. Sipping his beer and accepting a huge kiss on the cheek from his uncle, Dane's eyes evert towards the restrooms then back to Hazel. He wonders if she's alone or if someone with her is in the bathroom. Her long hair covers most of her face but he can tell she's striking and not from Melbye. He likes that.

A hush comes over the crowd as Trudy shouts at everyone, "Here it's on! Turn it up!"

The larger television shows a *Breaking News* segment in bright white and blue letters. Hazel squints and sees the words across the screen: Hero Fireman Rescues 3 Children and 1 Adult from Trailer Fire in Melbye. A segment of video shows him running from a side door of the home, tripping in his fire gear, falling and rolling with a young girl about seven years old, then standing again with her cradled to him and running again as the roof collapses. The video pans to the newscaster and the clip explains more of the details. Hazel sits back against the booth chewing. She's impressed by the guy. He seems to really know his job and none of the kids had even a scratch on them.

A handful of locals get up and go over hugging him and shaking his hand. Hazel admires his modesty while trying to accept each person's need to celebrate. His eyes move from an old man he's talking with to Hazel. She sees him, smiles, then looks away quickly. She doesn't want to seem as if she's prying.

■■Dane notices her reaction and finds he wants to go talk with her. She's tall, brunette, slender and looks as if she could take him away from all this with just a glance. He feels he's got to get a closer look at her eyes.

Hazel looks into her glass. The last of the beer can stay there. She's much too full to finish it. She decides to leave cash on the table before making her way towards the side exit. The celebration has moved into long off-key renditions of Irish songs befitting the name on the light-up bar sign of O'Tooleys. Trudy appears again from the bar and brings her another beer along with a small shot. She places them down in front of Hazel, takes her warm beer and plate, and turns walking back.

"Oh, uh-." Hazel tries to refuse.

6

Trudy turns speaking over her shoulder, "It's a welcome thing...from Hennie."

Hazel frowns slightly looking down at the alcohol she hadn't ordered. She's confused and also not sure who she'd be offending if she just got up and left it there. She certainly doesn't want to offend anyone in Melbye.

The door to the restroom shuts, her eyes meet his. The celebrated fireman emerges, drying his hands on a paper towel. One of the sorority girls skips over to him and wraps her arms around his waist hugging him tight.

"Uncle Dane!" She squeezes him and he kisses the top of her head. When she releases him he smiles handing her his paper towel while mouthing something to her.

His eyes lift and reach Hazel, his face softens. She notices he's gentle and loving. His face is freshly washed, the cut on his cheek looking less severe. Hazel likes the streaks of finger marks and water strewn through his dark brown hair. When his niece releases her hold, he pulls at the bottom of his shirt trying to straighten it, rubbing his hands on his jeans to further dry them. He walks around his niece and steps towards Hazel. She watches his eyes and notices their deep blue shade as he comes towards her table. He extends his hand and speaks deeply and calm.

"Dane Hennie."

Instinctively Hazel reaches to meet his grip, "Uh, Hazel." His voice makes her body react in unexplainable ways.

Dane smiles, he likes her voice. "May I join you?" He points to the empty booth across from her.

Hazel finds herself nodding before even knowing why. He's very charming with his peaceful nature and deep dimples. She watches him slide his large frame into the small seat, not quite fitting.

"Thank you. I need a break for a moment. I hope you don't mind." He points to the beer and the shot sitting in front of her. Hazel smiles noticing his energy feels nice.

"Ah, so this is you?" She raises her long fingers and points to the beverages.

He nods, his eyes softly admiring her closely. "I wanted to welcome you to Melbye. It's a thing."

"I'm pretty sure I should be buying you a drink." Her finger next points towards the television that revealed parts of his day a short while ago.

He chuckles, "Not at all. I was doing my job. My family tends to make a big deal of things sometimes."

Hazel finds his humility sexy. She suspects he'll divert the attention off himself.

"Where ya from Hazel?"

She blinks slow and smiles, "I'm from South Carolina. Myrna Beach area."

"Ah, could explain the tan."

"Tan? Oh, uh yeah."

He watches her look down at her arms. Her hair falls from behind her shoulders and covers her very appealing breasts tucked tastefully in a halter top. It's a beautiful shade of aqua and accents her bronze skin. She looks up at him and he feels his body react.

"Well, you're pretty sun-kissed yourself. Is that from uh..."

Hazel looks over to his fire crew, most are weathered in a pink shade, he's beautifully sun-kissed. She can smell the smoke across the table. It's nice. It smells like a bonfire every time the fan turns and wafts air in their direction.

He likes how her mind works, "Well, that's mostly sweat and bad choices on those guys." He chuckles. "The protection gear is brutal, so they tend to strip down while still on scene. I am *sun-kissed* as you say, but from kayaking mostly. Do you enjoy water...sports?"

"I do. I paddle-board and kayak depending on my mood. I enjoy a yacht here and there as well." she smiles, "and I've been known to go on cruises. Water is...*a thing*."

Hazel quiets realizing she's sharing a lot with him so quickly. Oddly, she feels ease talking to him. He has a gorgeous face and kind, deep set eyes. Her body is responding to his presence in strange ways. She squeezes her legs together to try and reset. Trudy flip-flops over to their table and serves Dane a beer and the same shot.

"There, now you're both equal!" She smiles and walks off, her pretty green toenail polish illuminated by the fluorescent whiskey sign on the wall.

Dane smiles and lifts the shot, "Cheers."

Hazel lifts her shot to his and clinks the tiny glasses before shooting it back. She normally doesn't day drink but with the stress of her grandmother's passing, the move, and a new handsome stranger in her midst, she figures what the hell. Expecting an intense aftertaste she braces herself, but surprisingly the shot is buttery and delicious!

Dane smiles wider, this time showing a full set of straight white teeth she can tell are natural. She admires them and his appetizing lips that stretch evenly over them. She can tell he's never had to bear the embarrassment of braces as she did. He's oblivious to his good looks.

"Yeah?" He nods questioning her opinion.

She smiles nodding back, "That was probably the best shot I've had in a long time."

"Right? It's my favorite."

"What is it?"

"A buttery nipple...sorry." He shrugs hoping not to have offended her. She's not easily put off by body parts or sexual words. She thinks sex is the best thing ever invented.

"Ohhhh, I like that." She puts her finger to her mouth to make sure not a drop has escaped.

"Want another?"

"No, nooo thank you. I'm good. I need to save my energy." Hazel picks up her beer smiling awkwardly, realizing how that came out. She feels she should elaborate. "For moving in I mean."

"Ah, are you joining us here in Melbye?"

She nods, "For a few months."

"For work...oh welcome, by the way. We're all crazy here but this is a town full of big hearts." Dane nods to the crowd at the bar surrounding his father, who seems like a wild red-faced Irishman, cracking jokes and telling tales.

"I'll be working, yes. I'm just not sure how long it will take me to finish my project. I'm thinking six months or so if things go smoothly."

"Sounds exciting."

"Not really. I'm a writer but this...*this* move is at the urging of my recently deceased grandmother. She made me promise to move here and research a book she asked me to write upon her passing."

Dane sits back against the booth, canting his head just slightly. "That sounds important Hazel, what a great promise to fulfill."

"I'm sorry...I'm completely dumping my *story* on you here...on your big day. Please-".

"No. No you're not, truly. I'm intrigued. And that stuff there, up on the flat screen, well that's my job. I like to fight fire. It's what I do. This party stuff is more for them...and my pops. It's a decent sized town and they look for any opportunity to party."

Dane smiles drinking his beer, his eyes glancing over towards his dad. Hazel could tell they were related straight away. There's no mistaking the good looks, Dane is just very buff. His dad is older, a tad shorter, and has a dad-bod belly. She can see he loves his father and is content with letting him soak up all the pride and attention his son brings forth.

"He seems to be very proud of you." She blinks slow, missing her grandmother's pride.

"He is. I'm his only son and followed in his steps. It was easy. He makes it fun. I hope I can always make him smile like that."

Hazel watches him take a long sip of beer. It's nice to hear a son speak of his father so kindly. She's betting there is no mother, that the two of them really leaned on each other in tough times and build a tremendous bond.

"Is he the chief?"

"Yes. Can you tell?" He huffs a laugh. He feels his father has a personality as big as the sky. He looks over and laughs

11

harder at the sight of his father's unbuttoned uniform shirt and disheveled happy-drunk look.

She searches his face, "Not easy being the chief's son is it?"

"Aw, it's not so bad. I mean as a kid you can't do anything wrong without everyone running to your dad, but I think Tracey Gordon had it worse. Her father was the chief of police."

"That could be a bit tougher."

"It was. Hey, so whereabouts are you moving here in Melbye? Have you found a place? I only ask because I'm renting the top floor of my house...and well, I don't think I could handle another band crew, with shift work and all, it wasn't a good fit." Dane's eyebrows furrow slightly.

Hazel huffs a laugh at his facial expression. She knows shift work is brutal on the body and trying to sleep when a band is practicing must be all the more so. "I have found a place thank you. I'm headed there now actually. It's on Renault Street? Are you familiar?"

His eyebrows raise, "I live on Renault! Ohhhhhh, are you moving into Linda Yerro's house? The little blue one?"

"Yes! You know it then?"

He nods, "The Yerro's are good people. Well, they were. Bill passed last year and I believe Linda told me she moved down south with her sister?" Dane is overjoyed to know he'll be able to see Hazel right from his porch and side windows. She's quite beautiful and he doesn't mind *seeing* her at all.

Hazel smiles, "Oh, that's great to hear. Linda wants me to buy the house but I told her I can rent for the six months and help her repair the house up so she can sell it. I've only planned my life up until then."

"Well, that's quite all right. I imagine you can go anywhere being a writer. It's kind of exciting. That's a career you can take with you no matter where you land right?"

"It is. I'm pretty happy with it. I've published a few novels that keep me financially comfortable. I was taking care of my grandmother until recently, but with her gone, I've no need to stay in South Carolina anymore. She insisted I not stay and anchor myself there. She was big on adventure, hence sending me on this one."

Hazel thinks to herself that she should stop sharing so much. He seems so easy to talk to. She sees her beer is almost gone and promises herself she'll get going soon.

"I'm sorry to hear of your loss, Hazel. You seemed close?"

"Thank you. We were, yes."

"Was she ill? I mean, if that's too personal-"

Dane realizes he's interested in her. He may need to reign in his questions so he doesn't seem intrusive. He thinks how nice it is to talk with a woman with a clever mind and one not trying to flirt so hard.

"She was towards the end. She had a weak heart. She was okay with it and very positive. I've never seen anyone love life here but be excited to *go on* as she put it. I hope to feel that way when I'm in my eighties."

He smiles, "Thats a good attitude. She sounds great Hazel."

"She really was. I lucked out."

He wants to ask about her family but realizes this isn't a date, even if he did sort of invite himself into her booth. He would love to take her out. He doesn't see any ring. It's hard to ascertain by her calm demeanor if she'd be interested. They did just meet. He can't recall every feeling so attracted to a woman so soon or wanting to...just talk. He sees her looking at her phone. He doesn't want her to go.

"I hope I'm not keeping you. I just wanted to welcome you to Melbye. Are you needing any help moving?"

She's beginning to think he likes her. It feels good. She doesn't really have to go. The longer she stays away the more the movers will get done on their own. She doesn't have many personal belongings since Gram insisted she only take what she cherished and use the inheritance to have a comfortable life. She bought furniture and wants to upgrade the kitchen for Mrs. Yerro. Sitting here talking with him feels more fun at the moment. The house stuff can wait.

"Thank you thats super thoughtful. I paid movers to do their thing. I'm just here keeping out of their way." Hazel shrugs and finishes her beer. The shot and beers are starting to feel good. Her joints are *warm and fuzzy* as Gram called it.

"Oh fantastic! How about another? Otherwise I'll have to go back to the crew over there and who knows what could happen." He smiles, making her laugh.

Just then the side door opens letting in too much sunlight. Dane squints, then moves his head to the side to get out of the brightness and focus on who entered. The door slams. He looks Crosby Sills up and down and nods without smiling. Crosby is Trudy's ex-husband, and Tommy the chef's, father. Not many turn or even acknowledge him. Hazel watches Dane's eyes, his smile fading.

A hand comes around and Dane puts his glass down to shake it. Hazel's eyes evert to a tattoo between the thumb and forefinger of the stranger's hand, her body reacts by freezing. Her breath hitches.

Crosby Sills' voice is nasally, not manly at all to her. She doesn't turn to look at him yet, "Hey Hennie, great job at that fire man."

Dane shakes quickly, releasing and nodding. "Thanks."

Crosby Sills turns to see who Dane is sitting across from and locks eyes with her as she lifts her gaze. He smiles without blinking and walks away trying to place her. He knows he's seen that beauty before. Hazel grabs her items and slides out of the booth leaving two twenties on the table.

"It was a pleasure meeting you Dane. I just remembered I'm late to pick something up before heading to the house. Thanks for the drinks."

Hazel turns and darts out the same door Crosby Sills just came in. Gone.

Chapter 2

Predator

"The best revenge my Hazel is to go on and be the greatness you are. He can never take that!"

H

azel drives her truck out of O'Tooley's bar vowing to never return! She can't believe that mother-fucking douchebag lives in the very town her grandmother sent her to, to fulfill a promise. Almost all of her wants to just keep on driving and never look back, but the tiniest part of her knows she can't let him win, *again*. That terrible night, back in college, begins to rush in flooding her mind with all that she's worked so hard to heal from. Gram's sweet southern voice comes to her and she hears her words that always kept her going:

"The best revenge, my Hazel, is to go on and be the greatness you are. He can never take that!"

She knows it's true. She knows Gram was *always* right. Hazel runs her hand down her face and slaps her own cheek trying to stop her C-PTSD brain from highjacking her awesome day. She was really enjoying getting to know Dane Hennie, then Sills came in. She feels bad about how she abruptly left Dane but her body completely tanked into fight-flight-and-freeze mode. She knows to remove herself from a situation when that happens. Everything in her wants to keep on driving out of Melbye and down to the Keys and maybe even out in the ocean so she can swim to Cuba! Crosby Sills is a predator and she despises him.

██ █

Crosby sits down on the farthest bar stool close to the wall. No one cares. No one acknowledges him. His ex-wife Trudy comes out from the kitchen and eye-rolls to herself as she sees him waiting. She hates when he waits at the bar. He expects free drinks. Tommy is a grown man and his father still sits on a bar stool waiting for him every Friday like it's his "weekend dad" time.

Trudy serves some food and swings around crouching under the bar slab, making eye contact, "Hey."

"Well, hey yourself Trud. You tell the boy his pops is here?"

"It's Friday Sills, he knows you're here. He'll clock out when his shift ends, get cleaned up, change his shirt. Same shit, different Friday."

Trudy walks down the other end of the bar to ask the fire crew if they need another round. The best things she can do is stay away from her ex. Her son is twenty-two and for twenty-one of those years she and Crosby have been oil and water. He's just one of those piece-of-shit-manipulator-deadbeat-dads in her eyes and he's never done anything much to change her mind. She'd regret meeting him altogether but then she wouldn't have had Tommy, so Crosby was good for that.

She'd heard about what a great soccer player he was and how he went to college on a full scholarship but then a knee injury killed his dreams. Of course she learned about that and what an asshole he'd become a little too late. She was already pregnant and couldn't know how bad things would get. She's convinced she made the worst mistake of her life marrying him and hoping a family would turn him around. Trudy learned the hard way that you can't give a man love or a family and expect him to appreciate it or do right by you. She's finally free of him but her son is still very much enmeshed with his father. She never says anything but Tommy can tell the town doesn't much care for his Dad.

Crosby stares at his ex-wife's ass and waits for a free beer. He purposely shows up twenty minutes before Tommy gets off shift just so he can get a free beer. He'd much prefer to eat dinner at O'Tooley's with Tommy every Friday but the kid doesn't want to stay at work to eat after cooking for everyone all day. He thinks about lighting up a cigarette so Trudy will bring him that beer. She hates when he makes trouble, but in his twisted mind she's the one forcing him to act out by not giving him what he wants.

His eyes travel up her frame and then over to fix on the firemen. They're all having a good time celebrating their golden boy, Dane Hennie, again. Since Dane was born he's been doing nothing but winning in life and Crosby sits watching him with yet another happy moment. He turns to see the booth Dane was sitting in. It's empty. The pretty woman, who looked familiar, is gone and Dane is back over with his father trying to get him to leave or at least eat something. He looks around wondering where she went.

Crosby pulls a pack of cigarettes out of his front pocket and places them down on the bar. He knows how to get what he wants and Trudy is purposely trying to ignore him. Soon he'll light up and start pissing everyone off, but it'll get him what he wants. He's not so sure how Dane will react though. He's still afraid of him as the guy is massive...and a do-gooder. He knows Dane would toss him out on his ass.

He stares again looking Dane up and down. That woman he was with was a knockout. All women want Dane Hennie but he hasn't been in a relationship since Wendy. It's annoying how he can even charm the new ones who float into town. Crosby rubs his head and picks up the pack of cigarettes to get one as Trudy still has her back turned and isn't remembering to get him a beer. He suddenly sees the woman's face in his mind again, the pretty one with long chocolate colored hair. It's starting to bug him because he can't place her. He knows those green eyes from somewhere.

Chapter 3
Welcome
"Welcome to the neighborhood Hazel!"

H

azel slumps down into what she knows will be her new favorite writing chair. It's plush and has an ottoman making it more like a chaise lounge. She likes that it's the size of a love seat and could fit two people, if they were snuggling and watching a movie. Although she doesn't watch much TV she faces the chair towards the flat screen up on the wall. Looking around the room she's feeling accomplished now that the furniture is all in place. It's been a long day and the physical exertion has done her well with keeping unpleasant memories off her mind. The doorbell rings.

She sees his large frame though the windows and wishes she had time to clean up. She's sweaty and in booty shorts since the AC is taking its' sweet time getting the house cool. Normally she'd just ignore the door but he is about the only person she knows in Melbye...and he makes her stomach feel excited in a good way. Hazel opens the door and smiles.

Dane Hennie has a portable drill box in his left hand with a bow on it and a bottle of Merlot in his right. His face lights up when he sees her and his chest feels full.

"Welcome to the neighborhood Hazel!" Dane's face is gorgeous and his hair is freshly washed. She admires how well he cleans up. His visit makes her feel relief unexpectedly.

"Aw, thanks friend. Did you get a day off from the fire stuff?" She opens the door wider and waves him in. He steps into her foyer looking around.

"I did. It's kind of a thing the day after a big scene. Time off to recoup."

"Oh, that's cool."

"Listen, I don't mean to impose. I just wanted you to feel welcome here on Renault Street. We're one of the coolest streets in Melbye." He huffs and hands her the gifts.

"Oh my, this is so nice. I love this drill and Merlot is my favorite. Share some?" Hazel nods towards the kitchen unusually comfortable with letting him into her new home further.

He sees her very short shorts and her long, tan legs emerging from under them. It's a no brainer to follow her lead thinking his truck can get washed some other time. "Uh well sure, if you're having some."

"I am. I mean it's five o'clock somewhere right?" She places the wine and drill down on the counter and begins opening drawers, hoping she's unpacked a corkscrew. "Try one of those barstools out and tell me if you think they're comfortable or not."

Dane does sit and is impressed that he fits on the large seat. He pulls out his keys and gives her a detachable utility knife that has an extendable cork screw portion. She smiles wide and he explains, "Part of the job...to have the right tools on one's person at all times."

She laughs thinking of how sexually she could comment but she doesn't know him all that well yet. He may not like how open-minded she can get. "I'm impressed!"

"Oh good. I was aiming to impress with my lil' knife tool." Dane looks into her eyes and lingers there, she makes him feel at home. He looks away and admires her dusty blue colored cabinets, he doesn't remember Mrs. Yerro's kitchen being quite so stylish. "And these cabinets, wow, those are really something." He gets up and walks around to put his hand on the stained wood.

Hazel likes that he approves. "Aren't they? I had them installed yesterday. A nice upgrade for Mrs. Yerro's house. I think it really brings the kitchen up to modern times, especially with the chrome hardware and stainless steel appliances to match."

"I agree. This is a bitchin' kitchen girl. Great job. I may have to look into sprucing up my place now. I like this blue."

"Thanks. Let me know if you do. I have an eye for color. They even have a brushed charcoal color that looks great against a white tile backsplash." She steps up on her tippy toes to reach two wine glasses she did manage to unpack, wash, and put on the highest shelf in the cabinet.

Dane watches to see if she needs his help. She reaches one and ends up pushing the other farther back. He steps in to help. He can feel the heat of her energy near him and finds his body reacting to her. He hands the second glass to her and softly closes the cabinet. She thanks him and pivots back to the island trying to ignore the ache deep within her. His scent is mesmerizing. He feels the same about hers.

He returns to the bar stool and watches how her slender hands pour the wine and her long arms extend to hand him his glass. He finds himself very attracted to her physically but knows better than to focus on just her external features.

"I do enjoy a nice black and white kitchen. I see there is this new finger print smudge free black appliances package at Lowe's they've been advertising. It's really hot."

"I know right? I love it, it's sort of brushed and not real obnoxiously shiny."

"Thats the best part. Not too flashy."

"Oh, I like your taste Dane. Let's go try out the new furniture I just placed in the living room. I want to see if it's wine worthy." She trots barefoot past him and he happily follows. Her hair is falling down in strands along her back and he finds he wants to reach out and touch it's softness. He likes the richness of her brunette colors and the length she's grown it to. Hazel chooses the chair and ottoman leaving him the couch and opposite love seat to choose for himself.

He sits on the couch closest to her chair and puts his arm up across the back, his wine glass balancing in his other hand on his leg. He looks around his eyebrows raised. "This is really nice, Hazel. This fabric is super soft!"

"You like it? It's like a velvety micro fiber. Not good for animal hair but it might hide a wine stain or two with this plum shade, right?" She giggles, happy that he's so attentive to detail.

"Well, I promise not to get any on your new furniture. This room is full of light, what a great space! Do you write in an office or..."

"I think so too. I'll probably be in here the most...err, in this chair writing the most." Hazel brings her long legs in and tucks them under her. She sips her wine and feels the warmth of the tannins loving the deep cherry and smokey flavors. She looks down in the glass admiring how delicious the wine is.

"Oh, you like to write stretched as opposed to sitting at a desk?" He thinks how he's the same.

"I do. Oh wow, that is good wine!"

He smiles. She answers the next question without missing a beat, "Yeah, I like to be spread out when I write, not so much sitting formally at a table or desk. College cured me of that."

"Oh yes, the formidable college years. I'm glad you like the wine. My friend owns a vineyard out in the hills. I love his wines and tried to pick one I thought you'd enjoy."

"Great choice. Thank you so much, I kind of needed a break. My body hurts from all the pushing and shifting of furniture and boxes. I feel muscles I didn't even know I had."

Dane laughs looking over her muscle structure. She's lovely. He thinks of what it would be like to workout at the gym with her. She'd be fun to talk with. He knows the other firemen would tease him relentlessly since they haven't seen him with a woman in years.

"I can commiserate after yesterday's rescue. It's interesting how we can workout every day of the week but try to move furniture or lift a human and your body acts as if it's never felt lactic acid before." He cants his head.

"Right? Like what the hell, body."

He looks over the room again, "I am enjoying your plush couch and the company. Thank you for having me in. I was going to leave your welcome gifts on your doorstep thinking you were out investigating for your book."

Hazel likes his thought pattern, he's considerate and remembers what she's shared. "Oh, I'm not ready to start work yet. I'm giving myself some time to get settled. I'll start writing again when I feel moved in."

"Sounds like a plan. So have you met any of your neighbors yet or am I the lucky first?"

She pats her leg and smooths her hand along her quad muscles, "That you are fine sir. I've not ventured out past my truck yet to even wave to a neighbor from the driveway. I see that the folks to my right have a pool with a screened in porch structure on it."

He nods, "Yes, that's Gertrude and Minnie Wichowski. They like to use their pool in the evenings. And that screen structure is what we call a birdcage."

Hazel raises her eyebrows impressed at how much he knows, "Oh and I'm assuming Minnie and..."

"Gertrude and Minnie are married yes. They'll be your favorite sixty-something lesbian neighbors but don't ever go over alone. Sweetest couple but make sure you bring along a friend so they won't try to *convince you* to stay the night if you know what I mean."

Hazel laughs out loud at his facial expressions as he tries to be cordial about their friendliness. She thinks he's just so beautiful. The way he tries to explain sensitive topic. How his eyes squint for a moment when he's trying to be respectful and elaborate.

He realizes he doesn't even know her orientation and hopes he hasn't offended her. "Or whatever, if..."

"I'll bring you along as my protective friend then." She smiles wide peering at him as she sips her wine. It's so warm going down, she's grateful he came by. She likes his energy and it's nice to know someone from Melbye already.

He smiles, "I'm sorry I was just assuming...I-"

"Oh no, it's quite all right. I know what you mean. I'm unattached, straight, and not interested in sleepovers with sweet sixty-year-olds." She chuckles.

He's so relieved, "Oh, oh I see. There's no....one?"

"A boyfriend or husband? No, not currently."

"Oh wow, me either. We have that in common." Dane takes another taste of his wine and relaxes.

"Yes, we do, don't we?" She likes what she hears and wants to keep the conversation going. "And on the other side? Do you know anything about that neighbor on my left or the ones across the street?"

He smiles, "Well, I'm in the white house with the teal shutters diagonally to you."

"You are!?" She's quickly excited. "The one with the awesome wrap-around porch and hammock?"

He likes how her face lights up, "That'd be me. There are two hammocks by the way, so don't hesitate to come by and swing away whenever you need. With my schedule, my porch isn't utilized nearly as much as it should be. I'd love if you could enjoy it. The sunsets are amazing from out there."

"Oh how nice. Thank you Dane. I may just do that."

He continues, "Now the neighbor to your left is Mr. Rodney Banks. He won't bother with you. He might wave if it's a holiday or something but don't expect much. Mr. Banks likes his alone time. I put his trash out for him if he forgets.

Sometimes his body hurts from war injuries if it rains and he'll forget to pull his cans to the curb so if you see me over there, I promise I'm not trespassing."

Hazel's really enjoying how he explains things, "That's really nice. Now what day is trash day?"

"Tuesdays. Monday nights if you're a planner." He laughs.

"Well, I will try to keep up. This house is much more manageable than my grandmother's. Seven bedrooms, four full bath farm houses are lovely in theory but quite a lot to keep going." She lays her head back against the chair remembering how much more stress she used to have. She's feeling grateful to be relaxing with him with all the past behind her.

Dane nods, "I agree. A house that size needs a large family taking care of it...everyone sharing in the responsibilities right?"

"So true. It hurt to let it go but Gram insisted it was time to be free of all that. I was able to sell to a foster agency so the house will go towards housing children who need it."

"Now that's a great way to pass on your grandmother's home. I'm sure she would be so happy with your decision." He smiles, praising her.

"Thank you, I think she would."

Dane moves to stand up, "Can I get you more wine? I think I'd like another glass."

"I'd like that yes, this is becoming one of my new favorites. Hey, have you eaten?" She stands, following him into the kitchen. She's enjoying their time together and doesn't want it to end to soon.

Dane looks back over his shoulder to answer her, "Actually no, I guess that would be a good idea with the second glass of wine. How about I get some takeout?"

She places her glass next to his so he can fill it. "Well, I'm not a chef or anything but I think I can whip us up something tasty. I was able to use this app on my phone to get some groceries delivered so the cabinets and refrigerator are well stocked. How would you feel about a few steaks, maybe some broccoli and garlic mashed potatoes?"

Dane thinks she's a gal after his own heart, "With this merlot? I think you are speaking my language. Can I help?"

"That could be fun. How about some tunes, maybe Queen? I can cook to some Bohemian Rhapsody."

Dane smiles wide. He can't deny, she's about the most interesting female he's talked to in years.

"I can definitely get some tunes going for you."

She smiles reaching into the refrigerator to grab some items. "Awesome. My phone is blue-toothed to those speakers in the living room. I've got an album on there titled "Enya's Writing Songs", just choose that one and we'll eventually get a Queen song."

Dane steps around the counter and closer to her to do as she instructs. "Sounds good."

"Dane, you wouldn't happen to know anything about new barbecue grills would you?" She knows it's a silly question him being a firefighter and all.

"Enya, you are really speaking my language now girl. Where did you come from again? South Carolina?" He chortles.

Chapter 4

Femur

"Human remains!"

C

huck Hennie stands at the bank of the Melbye Canal, hands on his hips, squinting from the afternoon sun. He watches the rescue crew pull the new recruit back into the boat ass-over-head and laughs out loud, puffs of cigar smoke wafting in the air above him. He's dripping wet from the humidity in the three o'clock Florida sun, but nothing beats watching his best friend's crew roast the new recruits. He misses the days of being razzed by his father and uncles grooming him as he entered the world of emergency services. He thinks of how proud he is to be the chief of Station #6, and he loves fire but he sure misses dredging water.

There's a commotion on the boat between the new recruits and the crew instructors. Chuck can't quite make out what's going on but the recruit in the water is holding something in his hand above his head and wading towards the bow of the boat. One of the instructors bends over and takes a long item from the recruit diver. A second instructor surfaces, removes his face gear and talks with the other instructors on the boat.

Chuck squints more trying to make out whats going on, they're too far into the deepest part of the canal for him to hear their words. The lead instructor, McCrory, turns and shouts. "Dayton with you Chief?"

Chuck looks up the bank towards his truck. Police Chief Ron Dayton parked his rig next to Chuck's about five minutes ago but hasn't exited the truck yet. He turns back and shouts, "On the phone McCrory!"

Brian McCrory shouts again, "We got a femur over here!"

"What?"

McCrory brings his hands up to cup around his mouth and shouts again, "Human remains!"

The cigar in Chuck Hennie's mouth falls to the ground as his feet turn running towards the trucks. He's got to get Dayton off the phone and get the authorities out to Melbye Canal. Yesterday's storm seems to have drudged up some human remains on the bottom of the canal.

Chapter 5

Smoldering Death

"Come, I'll show you my mess."

S

he picks up her cell and answers his call. Dane's number is fast becoming her favorite and after hanging out with him the last few days, she realizes she's beginning to look forward to their conversations.

"Hello?"

"Hey Compton, I was hoping you were there." Dane's happy he didn't get her voicemail.

She smiles into the phone, "Yep, still here. I think I'm just about done this chapter."

"Ah, that's gotta feel good. No more boxes and clutter?"

"Nope. So over that moving stuff. Hey, thanks for all the help. I really appreciate your time." She runs her hand through her hair to push it away from her face.

"My pleasure. Hey, you got a minute?'

"Yeah, of course. Anything for my moving slash coffee buddy." She puts her pencil down and leans back against the chair. Her lower back is sore but in a good way.

"How would you like to have dinner at my place tonight. I'm not sure if you're busy, it's kind of short notice, but I'm getting off shift here and I thought I'd pickup some groceries, a six pack, and we could relax in my hammocks after I murder some pasta in my kitchen?" He knows he could have presented it better but admittedly he's nervous. She's quiet which makes him babble more, "Or we could venture out to one of Melbye's seven restaurants if you prefer a real chef." He huffs.

Hazel smiles, excited for his offer. She really likes him, "You know, murder pasta sounds great for a Thursday...and a Melbye restaurant sounds great for a Saturday...if you're not working."

He likes that she's already thinking ahead through the weekend, "That's a plan I can do Hazel. See you in thirty?"

"You'll see me walking down your sidewalk from way over yonder." She giggles.

"I'll be lookin.'"

■■

Hazel feels butterflies in her stomach she tries to will away. She's enjoyed the time she's been spending with Dane over the last weeks. The dinner they cooked together at her place was so much fun and then meeting for coffee, at the tiny coffee shop on Leeler Street three times, proved to be memorable. Just sitting and talking with him about life is becoming the best parts of her days.

She clips her hair half up, half down and chooses a comfortable shorts romper and sandals since it's about eighty-nine degrees out. Moving swiftly through the house she finds her lipstick on the counter in the kitchen. Filling in her plump lips with the muted mauve color, she wipes the corners of her mouth using her reflection in the mirror on the wall. Making her way over to the refrigerator she grabs a bottle of wine and the cheesecake she whipped up earlier but didn't cut yet. She knows it'll go great after Dane's pasta. She smiles as she thinks of him. He hasn't kissed her yet, not that she hasn't wanted him to. He seems to really enjoy their time together and she knows she's beginning to trust him. He cracks jokes often, sends good morning and good evening texts, he even sends funny pics of his co-workers and shares hilarious pranks they play on each other at work. He's made her feel so welcome in her new town, despite that nightmare Crosby Sills. She's decided to begin searching for Merrill Clement in the next few days but first she wants to enjoy her first time at Dane's home. She feels a thrill inside and recognizes she's actually missed him.

Locking the door, she heads down her driveway, her hands occupied with the items. She crosses the street and walks along the sidewalk looking on admirably at Dane's gorgeous home. It's quite large with the prettiest porch on the street. She sees his truck in the driveway and the lights on inside, her stomach swirls again. A month ago, she'd never have thought she'd be walking down the sidewalk of Renault Street towards the house of Dane Hennie, Melbye's hero. She smiles wide and marvels at how strange life can be. She knows Grandma Elsie would be happy for her and pleased that she made it to the town she asked her to be in.

Hazel tries to knock on the door, but he opens it just as she lifts her hand. His face lights up to see her, "Oh hey, I was just coming out to set the table."

"Hi!" Hazel steps back to let him by.

"Can I?" He reaches to help her and takes the items. "Oh how nice, did you make this? I love cheesecake."

"I did. I'm happy to have you to share it with so it doesn't all end up on my hips." She laughs nervously as his freshly showered look and scent makes her slightly weak in the knees.

He continues along the porch over to where he's set up a tiny two-person bistro table and holds the cheesecake in one hand while lighting a candle with the other. "Hazel, cheesecake or not, your hips are wonderful."

"Thanks." She raises her eyebrows in response to his compliment. She watches him fix the place settings and position the cake to the side. His back and rib muscles show gorgeously through his tank top and his thighs are enormous, filling out the workout shorts he threw on. She likes his comfortable "at home" look and matching flip flops. He tends to dress nicely when he's out with her, but his relaxed attire shows a bit more of his sculpted muscle and skin. She bites her bottom lip watching him, liking how he mentioned that her hips please him.

"So, I got us beer but that wine looks way more appealing. What are you feeling?"

She loves both but sipping wine with him has proven to be much more relaxing, "I love both, we could do wine with dinner and a beer for dessert?"

"Oooh girl, I like your thinking!" He places his lighter in his shorts pocket and walks back towards her. His hand extends and she realizes she want his to touch her. As he reaches her he grabs the wine and uses his free hand to slide into hers, "Come, I'll show you my mess."

His touch is warm and she turns to follow him instinctively, surges of sexual energy shooting through her as she tries to walk. Her insides pulse unexpectedly and she realizes she desires him. He steps in first bringing her through the screen door. She gets hit with the aromas of garlic and Italian spices that swirl within her nose making her mouth water. She can't believe how immaculate and large his home is! It's superb and reflects his eccentric and hipster type tastes with smokey grays and electric blues. She sees a few life sized black and white fire scenes on art canvases along the walls, and finds herself letting his hand go to place herself in front of them. They're magnificent.

"Did you photograph these? They're stunning."

He loves that she appreciates his art, "I did actually. Sometimes I can catch a good flame or some smoke as it rises to the sky. I love the look of fire, how it can destroy but still be so beautiful."

She looks at him and sees his passion as he stares at the curve of the flames that are taller than she is in the canvas. "It is something. Like the ocean, beautiful but should be respected for its danger."

He stares into her eyes, she wants to look away because she feels he might see into her...then again, she wants him to see the real her. Dane feels safe to her. Safe in a way she hasn't been able to have. She wants desperately to be seen. To be told everything is going to be okay.

He agrees, "Yes, it is dangerous."

He wants to kiss her so badly, his heart aches. He hasn't told her but since the day he met her he's felt alive again. In a way he hasn't felt since Wendy and her mother left. The emptiness of the abandonment went away the day he saw Hazel sitting in the booth at O'Tooleys. He steps closer wanting to kiss her but unsure. He looks at the canvas she's closest to.

"This one I took after we put the fire out. It took us ninety-three minutes to fight this one. But finally it was out. This was its' smoldering death."

"That's a great name for your photo. We should title it "Smoldering Death" with Dane Hennie under it."

He smiles, "That would be something. I may just start titling my art. Here, let me show you more of my home."

Hazel watches him step around her and walk down the hall towards the kitchen. She thinks how masculine his home is, how clean and put together he is...and how she'd welcome him showing her much more of his *everything*.

Chapter 6

Pray

"We've got a bigger problem than money old man."

C

rosby turns his tow truck down the long driveway and accelerates towards the house set far back on the property. He hates the house still and remembers how happy he was leaving it and his mother's bad choices. College didn't turn out how he'd hoped but at least he never had to live with her and Merrill again. He sees the rundown three story plantation home with four pillars of cracked paint and chunks of material missing. The shrubbery is all overgrown. He wonders if the old drunk finally kicked the bucket. That could explain why he hadn't answered his cell phone.

Crosby hops down from the truck and slams the door loudly hoping to announce his arrival and avoid seeing the barrel of Merrill Clement's shotgun. Kruger comes running out. The old basset hound looks haggard and worn but his tail is wagging, a good sign. He's well fed so there's no chance of Merrill being dead upstairs in his recliner. Crosby bends down to greet Kruger.

"Thought I asked you not to come around, Sills." Merrill's gruff old voice bellows from the second level porch, his gun pointed up towards the sky for a change.

Crosby looks up at his former stepfather and spits a toothpick to the ground, "Actually you didn't ask you told me not to come around *ever*."

"Yeah, not like you ever listened."

"Well, I would have stayed away if you'd answer your phone."

Merrill steps away from the balcony. Crosby knows he'll come down because he doesn't want him to go inside.

Crosby finishes petting Kruger and stands up just in time to see Merril llimping out onto the front porch. He scuffles over to a rocking chair, his shot gun by his good leg. He sits without inviting Crosby to join him. "How much money you want now?"

"We've got a bigger problem than money, old man."

Merril huffs sarcastically, "What could be more important to you than money?"

Crosby lugs his workbooks up the front steps and positions himself on the front porch railing across from Merrill. He hikes a leg up to sit and takes out a cigarette and lights it. Merrill impatiently waits for him to ruin his day.

Crosby can smell the gin seeping off the old man and he's obviously not bathed or had a haircut in months, "A dispatcher friend of mine happened to mention that a rescue team training in the Melbye Canal discovered a femur."

"What the fuck do I care about that?"

"You should care, they uncover my mother's car or her or my sister's remains and link it to you, you're gonna be in a whole mess of trouble."

Merrill reaches for his gun and points it low towards Crosby's feet, "You need to get your skinny ass off my property

Sills before I get cranky. Why don't you go and use those last college brain cells you never done nothing with to figure out how you're gonna keep yourself out of this whole mess of trouble?"

"I wasn't responsible for them, just how they got there."

"I loved your mother! Now get off my porch you fucking piece of shit!" Merrill speaks through clenched teeth, his anger seething among the spit that flies out.

Crosby smiles, exhaling smoke on him as he stands up and turns his back to go. He knows the old drunk doesn't have the guts to shoot him. "How's that leg holding up?" He turns as he steps down each step slowly, "You don't think there'd be any of that leg's blood still in Mom's car do you...I mean after all these years?"

"You better pray there isn't."

Crosby gets to his truck and opens the door. He looks back, "I don't pray, Clement but you go right ahead. Gonna need it if they find more than a femur."

Merrill shouts angrily, feeling the effects of his gin being too far in the house, "I told you to burn it you stupid fuck!"

Chapter 7

Fire

"Wow, would you look at that horizon."

D

ane takes his last bite of cheesecake and closes his eyes showing blissful appreciation with a satisfied smile. "That was divine, Ms. Compton. I officially love your cheesecake with Oreo cookie crust."

Hazel is pleased. She sits back against the chair and kicks offer sandals. She brings her finger to her mouth watching him react to pleasure. He's lovely to watch, his lips are sexy when they chew...when they speak. She imagines how they'd feel on her skin.

"I'm happy you approve. This whole dinner was delicious! I love how food tastes outside."

"Right? Like French fries at a baseball game, or a hot dog with sauerkraut at a carnival."

She nods, "Yes! Oh and a warm pretzel from Philly with extra mustard on top."

"You've been to Philly? Like as in a Phillies game?"

"Yep, been to an Eagles game too."

Dane's enjoying their conversation as usual, "Oh, I'm jealous. I promised myself I'd visit the East coast someday. I just haven't had the chance yet."

"It's a must. I'd go with you. There's a few states I still need to cross off the list." She finishes her wine and Dane is ready with the bottle to pour her more.

"I'll take you up on that offer. Hey, how are you feeling? Ready to hangout in a hammock?"

She widens her eyes and nods eagerly, "I would love to stretch out after all that pasta!" Hazel stands up and skips like a child to where his two hammocks hang from the porch ceiling.

Dane loves seeing her playful side. He carries their wine glasses and watches here hop into the turquoise hammock leaving him the larger teal one. She sways slightly and snuggles in with a pretty smile pressed across her lips. He leans forward to hand her the wine glass. She raises her eyes to his and locks on. He feels his heart swell. He wants to touch her face reaching in but instead moves a strand of hair away from her mouth. He's still unsure how she feels and the last thing he ever wants is to cross her boundaries.

Hazel's eyes close for a moment, she's hoping he's going to caress her face. She feels the hair move across her lips and realizes he was helping her. The warmth of his large hand being so close to her skin makes her ache inside for him. She's unsure how he feels and doesn't want to ruin the friendship that's grown. He's become the most important person in her new life!

"Oh, thank you. My hair is all over the place with this humidity."

He moves his hand back and steps to the wall turning on a switch that turns on the ceiling fans. The breeze circulates and the coolness feels good on his skin. He looks back to her, "How's that?" His smile is so sweet.

She looks up wide-eyed and impressed with the Hemingway style fans, "Wow, you are full of solutions aren't you? That feels amazing! Do you ever sleep out here?"

"Believe me, I've thought about it from time to time but I do prefer air-conditioning at night, especially after a particularly rough shift. I have been known to nod off for a nap now and then if there aren't too many bugs."

"I can understand that."

"You all settled in?" He points to her as he walks towards the hammock next to her with his glass.

She nods, "I am. Get your butt in your hammock Mr. Hennie. The Hennie Heinie deserves a rest after such a fabulous meal." She giggles, almost nervous for showing her child-like side. She's feeling more and more comfortable around him, he's so easy to be with.

"Hennie Heinie?" He chuckles deep easing down into his hammock alongside of hers. "That's a new one!" His hammock sways after his six-foot-four frame stretches the length of it, causing him to bump into hers.

Hazel laughs and reaches to grab the edge of his hammock to hang on and sway together. Her hand grazes his and she moves it, "Oops, sorry about that." She's feeling giddy inside.

"That's quite all right Ms. Compton, you may hold onto me anytime."

She quiets at how lovely that sounded in the even air, tree frogs and cicadas singing from the trees in the backyard. His voice has a vibration that makes her body want to move in close. She says nothing.

Dane realizes he spoke instinctively. He looks forward, crossing his feet at the ankles. Hazel follows. They're both moving into closed body language unknowingly. She looks ahead seeing the setting sun glow beyond the view of their tan bare feet.

"Wow, would you look at that horizon."

"I never get tired of it. That's probably my favorite kind of fire right there."

"What, the sun?"

"Yes ma'am."

She looks over at him. He's her favorite kind of fire. "I guess it is the ultimate fire? There's nothing more intense than that of our earth's star." She huffs a laugh.

"You are correct, Hazel."

She hears the crunch of tires along the rocks of the driveway leading up to his porch. They both lift their heads up and peek over the porch railings. Chief Chuck Hennie, in a Fire Station #6 truck pulls in.

"My pops is here."

"Do you need me to go?" She hopes nothing is wrong.

He looks at her and frowns, "No way. Dad only stops by when he's got to fill me in on stuff or when I have him over for dinner. Otherwise he'd call. I did leave my phone on the counter in the kitchen though."

She smiles and relaxes. They can hear the scuff of boots walking up the porch steps. Dane doesn't get up so neither does she. They're both swaying, holding their wine glasses, relaxed, each with a pleasant smile. Hazel sees Mr. Hennie place his hand on the screen door handle ready to walk in.

"Dad?"

"Huh? Oh, there you are." He slowly hobbles, on sore feet, over to the far side of the porch. He notices her long legs and stops, then cautiously continues towards them. "Well, fuck me sideways, now I know why you weren't answering your cell son. How nice is this?"

Hazel smiles wanting to laugh at Chief Hennie's surprise. She smiles looking over at Dane. He smirks and rolls his eyes. He looks up at his father giving him a look, "Chuck Hennie meet Hazel Compton. Hazel, this is my Dad."

Hazel sits up to shake his hand, he steps closer to greet her, "No need to get up Ms. Compton. It's a pleasure to meet you lassie."

"So nice to meet you Mr. Hennie."

Dane wards off his father's coming interrogation, "Hazel is my new neighbor, she's renting Mrs. Yerro's house." He moves his thumb in the direction of the blue house just over his shoulder down the street.

Chuck Hennie looks over at the house then back at the two of them below him. He likes how handsome of a couple they make, "Oh my, well welcome to Melbye! You look slightly familiar Ms. Compton." His brows furrow as he tries to place her.

"Call me Hazel, please sir. I've been here only a few short weeks but I think you may have seen me at O'Tooleys?"

"Only if you call me Chuck, lil' darlin' and if I saw you at O'Tooley's, my apologies, I may not remember as I may not have been on my best behavior." He laughs heartily.

She laughs, "Well, I believe you were all celebrating a much deserved win against a trailer fire where children and an adult were rescued?"

"Ah yes! That was definitely a celebration. My boy here, the "Great Dane" what a day that was." He looks lovingly at his son.

Dane starts to get up, "Okay, okay. Dad can I get you a beer?" He hikes his body up and out of the spot he was enjoying with Hazel moments before.

"I don't mean to interrupt you two...uh, no to the beer because I have some more driving I have to do but could I bend your ear for a moment son?"

Dane smiles, knowing his Dad needs a favor or a shift covered, "Sure, how about a plate of pasta in the kitchen then Pops?"

"Well, okay then if you are insisting lad." He smiles at Hazel and moves towards his son who places his arm around his father's shoulders and guides him towards the door.

Dane looks past his father to Hazel, "Can I get you anything Hazel? Please enjoy the sunset, I'm going to feed this lil guy and I'll be back."

"No thank you, take your time, I'm enjoying this immensely!"

Dane winks at her and smiles, causing her heart to feel full in her chest.

Chapter 8

volkswagon

"A car? In the Melbye Canal?"

D

ane makes his father a plate of pasta and hands him a beer from the refrigerator.

"I'd pour you some wine but I don't want you falling asleep behind the wheel." He places the plate in front of him sitting at the counter.

"She's gonna be your wife son, I can feel it!" Chuck Hennie points a stubby finger up towards his son, his face soft and pleasant. He's happy Dane's found something real. He's been single since Wendy disappeared with her mother.

Dane smirks, "All right, all right. What's so pressing, old man?"

His father dives into the pasta, Dane can tell he's not eaten which means he's gone over his shift at work.

"I'm telling you son, a father knows."

"Pop..." Dane wants to get back to spending time with Hazel.

"Sorry, okay you may want to sit down for this." He nods his head to the side directing his son to sit beside him.

Dane presses his palms into the counter and leans towards his father, he exhales long. "Dad, I have a very important guest over."

Chuck chews, "Yeah, I'm sorry about that. Listen, I just don't want you to be blind-sided tomorrow when you get to work before me. I wanted to tell you in person."

"Okay."

"I was out earlier today watching the rescue team train the two new guys...over at Melbye Canal?"

Dane takes a wash rag and begins wiping down the counter, "Right."

"One of the fuckin' recruits found a femur while down in the canal. Looks like the storm kicked up some remains."

Dane stops and stares at his father, "They know it's human?"

"It's human, son."

"Huh."

"And son, the young tyke says there's a car down there."

"A car? In the Melbye Canal?"

"A Volkswagen, son..."

Chapter 9

Tommy Boy
"What'd you do now Dad?"

C

rosby picks up his cell while waiting at a light. The convertible Buick next to his truck sounds busy with young female laughter. He puts the cell to his ear and looks over at them. A group of four college girls are dancing to a song with too much bass. He waits for his son to pick up the phone and smiles at the good time being had by the twenty-somethings only feet away from him. He thinks about his college days many years ago up on South Carolina. It was a wild time...until it wasn't.

Tommy doesn't answer as usual, so Crosby does his *usual* and recalls him. The stoplight changes to green and he lets the girls dart ahead of him. As suspected the bumper sticker on the back of their care reveals they go to the university on Brenner Road just five miles ahead. Listening to another ring to his son's unanswered cell, he dreams in his head of sitting sandwiched between all that young pussy. He remembers how easy it was to do as he pleased with whoever he chose at college. So many of the girls were too trusting, too drunk, and way too far away from any family sense or morals. Back then it was all so easy...until, of course, that one incident. He reluctantly remembers, accelerating to catch up to the convertible ahead with mounds of long hair flying in the air, arms raised up dancing in time with the drums of the song. Annoyed, he hangs up and dials once more. He knows if he keeps it up he'll get his son to pick up. If anything, he knows how to force what he wants.

Merrill Clement crosses his mind again. Crosby thinks how the old bastard isn't as high strung as he once was and that's not good. He doesn't seem to care about being linked to the disappearance of Regina and Wendy eight years ago. He's old, and Crosby knows if he doesn't give a shit about going to jail for killing his mother and sister in the drunk driving accident, he's certainly not going to care about indicating him as an accessory. Crosby slams his hand against the wheel cursing his former stepfather. If he hadn't owed him for the college cover up, he knows Clement would have had to dispose of the bodies and car himself! Crosby fumes that the drunk old fuck of a college dean drunk is going to probably throw him out to pasture, let him take the fall, and he'll just drink himself to death and never see the inside of a prison cell.

He feels evil and thinks about running up on the girl's convertible bumper to maybe having a little fun scaring them. It's been a long time since he's felt the rush of scaring a young girl...or a few. Tommy finally picks up during the fourth ring of his third attempt.

"Dad!"

"Yo son."

"Dad, I'm working. I told you, if I don't pick up I'M WORKING. I'll call you back when I can. You're going to get me in trouble." His son is half-whispering.

Crosby smiles, loving the attention of NOT doing what his son had requested. "Your boss is your mother kid, how much trouble could you get into? Now knock off the "grab-ass" and listen to me for a second."

"Dad!"

"Tommy Boy, I'm fuckin' telling you just give me a goddamn second!" Crosby pretends to lose his temper so he can control the conversation.

Tommy hates how much of a bully his father is, "Make it quick."

"I'm heading out of town for a bit."

"What'd you do now, Dad?"

"Don't be a dick Tom, I just have to take care of some things for my boss. Like car hauling shit. Might take me a few weeks. I just wanted to let you know."

"For how long?"

Crosby purses his lips, "I don't know man, it's across states and involves deliveries and shit. I won't be able to do dinners for a while."

"Yeah okay. Well, call me when you get...when you get back."

"Will do. Hey, you nail that split-tail who keeps coming into your work and blowing you kisses?"

Tommy exhales loudly, "Dad, you should have more respect for Dane Hennie's niece. She's a good person."

"Yeah right, okaaaaaay son."

"That man would kill you if he knew you were disrespecting Jennifer like that, Pops."

Crosby cackles, "Sure son, okay. I won't say anything more about Jenny Hennie then."

"I didn't see you saying too much when he escorted you out of O'Tooleys the other week. I told you not to come early to pick me up from work. I'll meet you somewhere. Mom's not gonna put up with your shit forever. Why can't you just stop being so difficult?" Tommy huffs impatience towards his father.

"You know what Tommy Boy, why don't you go whine to your mommy and call me when you learn to respect your father okay?" He pushes the end button and throws his cell against he seat. Crosby runs up on the bumper of the group of girls in front of him, then lets up causing them to scream and speed up trying to get away from his truck. He laughs thinking how if he didn't have to head out to the swamp to hideout in the cabin, he'd run them into the ditch and maybe even fuck one or two of them, especially if they were knocked out. He always loved fucking girls who were dumb enough to black out...or better yet lose consciousness.

Crosby checks the rearview mirror and looks around, his predator instincts tell him it's too risky to play with this group of rich, entitled brats although he wouldn't mind taking just one of them to the cabin. He knows he'll have to think of something if he's going to live there for a while. He imagines borrowing his son's crush just to get back at her Uncle Dane for forcing him out of O'Toolers a few weeks back. Dane Hennie pisses him off. If he only knew what happened to his precious Wendy all those years ago, he might not be so great in everyone's eyes. The town hero dating his sister all those years was annoying. He wonders what goodie-two-shoes Dane Hennie would do to Merrill Clement if he knew Wendy never left him after their little breakup fight, that her own father killed her and his wife while driving them drunk.

He sees the young girls up ahead pulling into a gas station. He doesn't need any witnesses so he raises his arm pretending to fix his hat and covering his face as he blows by them. He chuckles at how scared they are. They'll never give an accurate description so he's not worried about it and his license plates are for the wrong vehicle anyway so they won't get anywhere tattling.

Crosby erases them from his mind. He's no longer amused. His mind wanders to having to spend the coming weeks hiding out at the cabin. He'll need to watch the case closely. If they track him down and he becomes a suspect, he knows he'll need to take off to a different country. He's pissed. This isn't going to be easy. He reaches to turn off his cell so it doesn't ping off the cell towers much longer. He has a burner phone to use and call Freddie for updates. It pays to have a friend who works in dispatch who also likes young girls.

Crosby leans his elbow on the door balancing his hand on the steering wheel while the other searches for a cigarette and lighter from his front pocket. Turning onto the hidden dirt road, he thinks about his stepfather. *Merrill Clement, former Dean of Fenny College.* He considers how a suicide could help. If the case starts to get too heavy, he knows he can throw the authorities off his scent by "helping" Merrill confess. A suicide note from a has-been drunk dean apologizing for the deaths of his wife and daughter would close the case quick. Crosby smiles at how he might even get some money out of it. He'd at the very least, get sympathies from everyone in Melbye.

He lights a cigarette thinking about how all this could go in his favor. Life may take a turn for the better. He just has to stay away from women. He smiles. He's done too many things to too many in his past. He needs to keep away from them...especially the twenty-somethings at the university nearby.

Chapter 10

Unsure

"I don't want us to stop what feels right."

H

azel enters the screen door cautiously. She waved goodbye to Chuck, but, when Dane didn't come out to join her in the hammocks again she figured she should check on him. Looking around she doesn't hear him. She steps barefoot through the hall passed the gorgeous art towards the glow of the kitchen light. There, sitting with his head in his hands is the man who makes her heart skip a beat. He turns to see her, his eyes sad. She's unsure how to approach him. He tries to smile and as he begins to try to stand she instinctively steps to him. Without words she opens her arms to him and he takes her gesture as invitation and falls into a hug tight within her embrace. Hazel can feel his desperation and yet her body fires off in pulses of attraction wanting all of him. He exhales deep into her hair his large frame towering over her. She loves the feel of his body pressed up against hers. He's warm and enticing, his musk scent swirls around her making her feel as safe. She yearns for more. She realizes there is no going back to friends after this. Her body burns for him. She knows she wants more from him now. She's wanted him since the first moment she laid eyes on him.

Dane thinks she feels like heaven in his arms. The smell of her hair covering his face entices him to kiss her neck, but he holds back. His body reacts, his manhood aching deep within to be inside her. He's wanted this, her...to open up to him. He hates that its right after his father told him Wendy and her mother's car may be sitting at the bottom of Melbye Canal. He feels awful. Then again, he feels he wants to go back to the moments before knew. He wants to allow this moment to be what it is. He feels her stir.

Hazel whispers, "I'm hoping everything is okay?"

"It is now. Thank you." He pulls away and looks down into her wanting green eyes. He sees her compassion for him.

Hazel stares into him, his eyes saddened yet desirous. She has no idea what to do next but she knows she's very pleased she let herself touch him in this way. Her arms are resting on his biceps, she likes how her hands look touching his skin. She moves her hands up along his shoulders and reaches up to run her hands into his hair. Dane closes his eyes slowly absorbing the pleasure of her touch, his instinct to lean into her hands. He's wanted her touch for weeks. He knows she's more important that the news he just heard from his father. All this time he thought Wendy left him. Just took off with her mother, the two of them living it up in Vegas like Crosby mentioned. He doesn't want to think about all the hurt he felt, all the pain he went through thinking Wendy didn't want him anymore after that last fight...and how none of it was true if she's at the bottom of Melbye Canal.

Dane opens his eyes to look at Hazel. She's so much more important right now. She's the present, Wendy is the past. He brings his hand up to cup her cheek, her long hair caresses his forearm. It tickles yet arouses too. He thinks she's so alluring. He decides he's going to try. He has to at least let her know how he feels in the moment. He leans down unsure, Hazel finally sees what she's been hoping for all these times they've been together. He wants to kiss her. *Finally*. She moves in and meets his lips. His mouth is warm and tender just as he is. She exhales feeling as if everything all makes sense now. He moves his tongue slowly towards her wanting mouth. She loves how he kisses. She accepts and gives to him equal connection. Her tongue eager to explore his. Their bodies melt into each other and an intense energy surges through them. Dane embraces her further and deepens the kiss. Hazel loves how he feels strong and safe, she easily molds to him and turns her head slightly to deepen their reverence. She spreads her hands along his large back and presses them into him. He moves his hand to the small of her back, the other to the back of her neck tenderly, holding her to him. Hazel feels as if she never wants him to let go of her. His lips are sweet and fevered, the taste of him magical. She presses closer and feels him growing firm against her stomach. It arouses her beyond words, she loves that he wants her. Suddenly he releases his hands.

"I- I guess we should stop?" Dane is unsure.

She looks into his eyes and sees he's being the gentleman he's been since she met him. She knows his body wants her as much as she wants him but his mind is unsure. He doesn't want to overstep.

She decides for them, "No, no....I don't think we should Dane. I've wanted you from the moment you sat across from me in that booth. I don't want us to stop what feels right."

Chapter 11

Thrusts

"Then don't."

H

azel stares up into his eyes, she spreads her fingers and strokes down his broad chest. He towers over her, his hands caressing along the sides of her breasts. Hazel closes her eyes as his touch sends pleasure coursing through her entire body. She feels herself getting wet, a moistness forming at her vulva entry that started deep within as they kissed in the kitchen. Dane has an almost electric touch that ignites parts in her she's forgotten. She wraps her hands down and around his waist pulling him into her. The feel of his shaft, long and warm along her hip sends pulses inside her womb. She wants him deep within her sacredness.

Dane brings his hands up under her ears to cup her face and plunge his tongue into her mouth again...sweetly, but with desire. He wants her more than he knows how to explain, he's letting his body show her how he feels. He leans her towards the bed and she pulls him down and on top of her as they rest on the soft mattress. The weight of him on her feels incredible and as much as she wants to do all sorts of oral things to him she aches so bad for him to enter her slick and waiting yoni. Dane likes how she opens up to him and pulls him to her opening without breaking their kiss. Her hands wrap farther around him and she pulls at his tush clearly consenting to him entering her.

He slides his penis head to her opening and moves slowly up and down lubricating with her slick fluids on them both. Hazel loves how he taunts and prepares her. She can tell he's considerate of her body and unrushed when it comes to important details. She brings her legs around him and uses them to pull him into her. Both of them moan in unison at the intense feeling of uniting for the first time. His enlarged manhood glides in long and hard, filling her entirely. Hazel grasps at his back as he sends pure ecstasy into her and through her every body cell. He inhales trying to catch his breath but not break the kiss. She engulfs him, surrounding him with her hot, slick womb and he can't believe the shear pleasure of her. He needs her so much and she wants him. Her desire is coming through. The feel of her grasp, her breathing, her deep, tender kissing...

Dane releases slightly and thrusts in deeper, Hazel moans again unable to believe the feel of his girth and how good he is as he presses in and then let's go just enough. She accepts him deep and then squeezes him tight bringing her hips in to meet him. Again...and again, he leisurely impales into her wanting body, the pleasure almost unbelievable. She can feel all of him.

Dane presses his forearms down into the bed to lift up and break their kiss so he can create more enjoyment for her. He trails kisses down her neck, across her chest, and finally onto her wanting nipple as he continues his rhythmic play below the waist. Hazel arches into his sultry lips. He's so tender with her nipple. He suckles and slowly glides his tongue around her areola before taking it all in his mouth, flicking softly but teasingly. He trails over to the other, giving it equal attention. She feels almost mad with want for more. Dane hears her moan into the quiet of his bedroom causing his manhood to pulse inside her as he thrusts. He's trying to hold off his orgasm so they can both enjoy more of their perfect evening. The way her body pulls him in is marring his concentration. Knowing now how she's wanted him as he her is arousing him beyond what he imagined. It's been so long since he's felt a woman make love to him. He's proud he's waited for Hazel. He doesn't want this feeling to end. She feels right. Her body yearns as does his, the balance he feels between them is extraordinary. Since meeting her he's imagined her in his embrace many nights but, this far exceeds what he'd felt in his dreams.

Hazel feels as if her body is taking over. She brings her hands up to run her fingers in his hair. He's moved on to her neck, his mouth-play sending waves of pleasure that circle down into her insides. She's trying so hard not to cum but he's overtaking her. Almost breathless she pulls his hair gently to lift his head up to her. Her mouth finds his neck and she begins to suckle and nibble wanting to devour him. Dane feels complete rapture and can't help but let out a deep exhale. He thinks she's magnificent. She's hungry with desire, animalistic in her moves and he loves it.

Hazel feels the beginnings of her orgasm, her body preparing to convulse with long awaited bliss. She moves her mouth from him and whispers, "Dane...I, I can't-"

He can feel her body respond to his deep thrusts, her legs tensing around him. He brings his mouth up to hers, "Then don't." He then kisses her forcefully knowing she's there. He takes her increasing their pace, bringing her with him as he lets go too...

Chapter 12

Ecstacy

"Admittedly, I've wanted this for a while now."

H

azel lays extended along his lengthy body. One leg draped on him, her arm trickling caressing fingers down his taut stomach. She feels the ripples of his ab muscles as he moves with breath. Dane reaches over to the nightstand and opens the drawer reaching in for a lighter. She watches as he flicks the lighter a few times then lights a candle with a wick that's never been used before. She likes how confident he is around fire. It makes her feel safe. He tosses the lighter in the drawer and closes it, turning his attention back onto her.

"There, now I can see your beauty in the dark." He whispers reaching to caress her upper arm. He likes the feel of her body up against him, she is perfect to him.

She smiles, her cheek against his chest, "I can see you better as well. Who knew you had all this sexy under those clothes all this time I'd been hanging out with you." She teases.

"You're very kind." Her comment makes him feel good. "I'd hoped to see that sunset with you earlier."

"It was a lovely sunset."

"My apologies that you were left so long alone, I hope to catch the next one. Perhaps sunrise will do?"

She laughs, "I do like the sounds of that. Is that your way of telling me I shouldn't leave?" She'd been wondering if she should head home. "It is...I'd like you to stay the night if you're up to it."

"Oh...I am soooo up to it." She giggles and he smiles at the feel of her breath against his skin.

The room is charming and falls quiet with only the sounds of the central air humming softly above. She wants to ask about his father's visit but feels it may ruin their moment.

Dane brings his hand and rubs his forehead, "Hazel, that...was incredible." He feels he needs her to understand how much he wants her near him.

"I agree. Admittedly, I've wanted this for a while now."

"I wasn't sure. I didn't want to make you uncomfortable. I've wanted to kiss you every damn time we've been together...especially before we'd part."

She circles her index finger softly on the skin of his pecs and down his ribs, "I've wanted that too, but didn't know where you are in your life with relationships. Getting to know you has been my favorite part of Melbye. It's been gradual...in a good way. My body didn't understand though." She chuckles.

Dane reaches for her face and turns to kiss her sweetly. "I've been enjoying our journey so much. I look forward to talking with you and spending time with you. My body, in all honesty, has been quite pissed with me. That head and heart thing aren't always easy for me."

"Well, let's hope we've helped balance things slightly. There's no rush here." She kisses him now, slowly and tenderly.

Dane reciprocates and feels a twinge of ache for her again. She parts his lips and finds his soft, wanting tongue. He glides along her tongue so gradually, he feels like velvet. Tasting him is magical to her. Her body ignites again. Hazel reaches her hand up and around his neck to deepen the kiss, communicating that she wants him again. He feels himself growing, desire welling up once more. She's fire to him and he's extremely attracted to her. His body wants her, wants to bury into her once more and further explore their new connection.

Hazel feels a familiar ache he ignites deep within her yoni. She desires him inside her again, her body pulses confirming it. No man has ever affected her like this and in the same night.

Dane moves his palms down her back to her waist and then slides them slowly around to her plump tush, grasping her and pulling her into his erection. He presses her clit firmly and she groans into his mouth. He realizes she's as aroused as he is, a match for his sexual appetite and he loves it. He breaks the kiss and moves her onto her back as he trails kisses tenderly down her neck, chest, and breasts. Continuing on to her tummy, he suckles lightly. Hazel moves her head back closing her eyes feeling his warm mouth on her skin. His thumb trails along her nipple as his mouth begins to explore lower, reaching her soft hair. Hazel gets excited as his mouth reaches her mound, the anticipation driving her mad.

He loves the feel of her below him and feels even more aroused that she's responding so eagerly to his oral pleasure. Opening her legs he sees how gorgeous her body is displayed before him in the candlelight. Her breath is labored and she's engorged around the opening of her sex. Her scent drives him wild and he tenderly reaches in to sweetly suckle at the hood of her most sensitive area. The pleasure is maddening and Hazel folds inward towards him, a cry of indulgence escaping into the air of the bedroom. She loves how he gradually moves his mouth and lips along with his tongue to delight her. When he moves his hands along his mouth to massage her folds and surrounding vulva, she feels as if she might lose control. Hazel has never felt a man so skilled. He's enjoying the feel of her lips and silky crevices beneath his lips and fingers. He moves his two fingers into her wet opening, increasing the sensations. Hazel inhales deep as his long tender digits sink deep and then curve to find her begging g-spot. He begins to move ever so slightly forming a C and she gasps in response to his instinctive knowledge of her erogenous zone.

Hazel brings her hands down and into his hair, loving how perfectly snug he fits between her thighs. She can't help but arch her back, her head reaching up as she tries to hold on. Dane knows she's trying to stop herself from letting loose but he wants her to know with him she doesn't have to hold back. He increases his oral rhythm and matches it to her labored breathing, syncing his fingers as well. Reaching just slightly deeper he presses his remaining bent fingers up against her anal opening taking her to yet a deeper level. She clenches around his hand and he knows she's close, she just has to allow herself his rapture. He softens his lips and allows his tongue to suckle a bit more while letting a moan escape in appreciation for her exquisite taste. Hazel can take it no longer and succumbs to the convulsions of her impending orgasm. Her body seizes and her breathing hitches as he takes total control of letting her crash into waves of ecstasy. Never has she been with a man like Dane.

Chapter 13

Our time

"I want you Dane."

H

azel guides Dane up her body. He releases his mouth and fingers realizing her body language is coaxing him up on top of her. He kisses her stomach and breasts as he maneuvers towards her mouth. She grasps him tightly at his shoulders wanting to feel him again deep inside her. The pleasure he gives is like no other and despite the hours of the night passing she doesn't want dawn to come too soon.

She looks into his eyes, "I want you Dane."

He smiles, enjoying her insatiable hunger. "Absolutely."

Whispering it into her ear and moving between her legs to satisfy her request. He touches her at her opening with his cock and waits for her to move towards him. She uses her hands to pull him by his waist and he enters and slides into her slickness. He feels her nestle around him snug as he buries himself as deep as she likes. Hazel holds him there feeling his length while moving her mouth to find his lips. He rests inside of her, feeling her clenched around him and then tighten and release. He kisses her slowly knowing there's no need to rush. He's decided in his mind he's going to call out of work and spend the entire next day in bed getting to know Hazel. For now though, he wants her satiated.

She begins to move and rock with him. She loves his slow, torturous pace because she can feel all of him. He speaks hushed, his voice gruff making her almost weak.

"This is..." He pauses, feeling her pulse and squeeze around him. He's never experienced such a passionate, responsive woman. "Hazel, you...are...*lovely*..."

His admission makes her want to explode around him again. He makes her feel so desired.

She twists suddenly and has him on his back before he knows it. She releases from him and moves down his body sinking her soft mouth down onto his rigid cock. He moans into the room, the pleasure almost more than he can stand. He had no warning but the exquisite feel of her mouth is a breathtaking surprise. She's so gentle and slow. Down..then up...d o w n...and slowly up again. Her tongue, her lips, everything is so loving.

Hazel reaches up to caress his chest and nipples creating streams of pleasure that coarse through his entire body. He feels as if he may go mad, not knowing what to do with his hands he runs them through his hair, his breathing hitching in his chest. Her mouth moves down his entire shaft inch by gradual inch again, she retracts suckling and causing every nerve ending to ignite in waves of ecstasy. Bringing her hands down she uses one to caress his scrotum pleasingly and the other around the base of his shaft to add more to his *bliss,* all without losing the relaxed rhythm he's now breathing into.

Dane's head arches back and he brings his hands forward gently to her hair. She can feel he's getting close, his body tensing. She loves giving him reason. But he wants to feel her again.

He sits up gently and climbs towards her, she likes how swiftly he moves and allows him to *take* her. Plunging into her readied, moist warmth, Dane thrusts easily as she's soaked with want for him. She's so wet with desire and he wants all of her. Thrusting again deep and holding at her clit, she cries out in pleasure. He buries himself again and again inside her begging womb, his lips to hers as they both try not to scream. The intensity of their connection creating more and more energy, they both increase the pace. Hazel moans into his mouth feeling his vehemence and accepting all of him over...and over...and over. He feels so fucking good.

She grabs his back hanging on. His weight is perfect for pressing into he and she loves how he holds for a torturous moment on her clitoris. He's big but tender and intense. He fills her and satisfies every bit of her.

"Hazel...oh my g o d..." Dane thrusts again...and again and she matches his rhythm, squeezing him inside and taunting him for more. She can hardly find her breath, the pleasure he's invoking through her body makes her feel as if she's floating. He's so *good*.

Dane continues thrusting, slowly flicking her clit at the end of each long push, matching her breath with his own. She feels her climax coming on strong almost as if she has lost all control. He's taking over her body and she likes it. She submits to his hunger willingly.

His body begins to slow. He leans up on his forearms holding her face between his palms. He looks into her eyes, holding her gaze as his lower body is taunting and burying himself slowly and rhythmically into her moist heat. He pushes deeper watching her, her head arches back and her eyes close, she loves how he's making love to her and he adores how she looks when pleasured.

She brings her gaze back down to him and sees he's very serious and trying to hold on for her. He has amazing control and cares about her as much as his own pleasure.

Dane slows leaning down kissing her, he retracts caressing the sides of her temples with his thumbs. His eyes are wanting, his body still teasing her below...over and over...and

"I-" Hazel tries to speak.

He plunges again holding himself to her clit, then scooping his hips before thrusting again. He understands the dance and what a woman needs. Hazel moans into the quiet of the room unable to control her body anymore. He's possessing her, taking her...

"You?..." He smiles seductively and waits for her to finish her sentence.

"I'm really enjoying *our*...time together."

Dane smiles wider upon hearing her words. His mouth comes down hard on hers, his body speeding slightly, his movements intensifying again as he begins his enchanting sorcery she learning to need and love.

Hazel feels she can no longer hold on and desperately grabs his back digging her fingers in, wrapping her legs around him. He knows he can bring them both into freedom...into a new level of connection together.

And...so he does.

Chapter 14

Twenty-three

"I don't want to bother him with it at work."

M

errill Clement stands at the edge of his porch steps watching the dust of dirt her car produces approaching his house from his long driveway. He never did get around to paving that road. He likes how Mandy is right on time just as she is every Saturday with his groceries. She pulls in and turns off the engine to her now *very* dusty Sentra.

Climbing out of her car she waves to him, "Hey Mr. Clement! How's this week been for ya?" She opens her trunk and collects his bags of groceries.

He raises his gruff voice, "Can't complain Mandy. I'm still kickin.'"

She laughs slamming her trunk closed and walks around the car to the steps. Merrill turns and limps back to the screen door opening it to let her in. He follows in after her and then down the long hall to the kitchen. He loves how her ass looks in her jeans. Kruger comes trotting towards her. He loves Mandy so there is no warning barks.

"Hey there, Kruger. I've got a surprise for you buddy." She places all the bags down and searches through a few of them until she finds the rawhide chew she brought for him. Kruger wags his tail at his favorite female, the only female he's *seen* in years.

Merrill slumps down in the living room recliner watching Mandy love on Kruger, then unload the bags.

"Thanks for bringing my order again Mandy, you're a lifesaver."

"We do what we can to help Mr. Clement. I actually enjoy the ride and I like to make sure you and Kruger are well. Haven't seen much of you in town this year, not even at the council meetings."

Merrill scratches his head, "Yeah, I haven't felt much like dealing with them assholes anymore, too many liberals."

Mandy smiles not taking offense, "Well, if you need a ride let me know."

"I do need your help with a letter if you can."

"Sure thing. Do you need it delivered or just put in the mailbox?" She finishes putting his groceries away and throws the bags in his top drawer.

Merrill reaches for the sealed envelope hoping it looks important, "Do you know Dane Hennie?"

"Everyone knows "Great Dane". She smiles wishing she knew him on a deeper, more sexual level. "He's about the most selfless, caring guy ever..."

"Yeah...well, I was hoping you could get this to him?" Merrill lifts a large envelop to her with only "Dane Hennie" written on the front. It took him all week to hand write the twenty-three page confession and he wants it gone before he changes his mind about it.

Mandy walks around the furniture and takes it so he doesn't try to stand on his bad leg. "I sure will, Station #6 is on my way home so I'll drop it there. He's probably on shift."

"Well, is there anyway you can give it to him when he's not working? I don't want to bother him with it at work."

Mandy stares down at Merrill, "Oh...oh okay, yeah. He lives over on Renault I think, I'll drop it by at his home then."

"I do so appreciate that honey, oh and here, there's an extra hundred in there for your troubles." Merrill points to her cash over on the counter.

"Oh wow Mr. Clement, that's too much!"

"No, it's not now stop that. Don't deprive an old man of how he wants to spend his money." He wags a finger at her while balancing both his hands atop his cane.

Mandy Simpkey feels somewhat guilty because she'd deliver the envelope to Dane for free just to get a glimpse of Melbye's finest up close and personal, "Well okay then but, I'll be bringing Kruger double the treats next week."

"Thank you Mandy. And I'm sure Kruger will approve. If anything should ever happen to me...you know, I'm not getting any younger and all well, I would hope Kruger could find a good home with you." Merrill tries to smile.

"Of course! Kruger is my buddy."

He tries to smile and hopes Mandy will be on her way soon. He's got some drinking to catch up on. A lot of drinking.

Chapter 15

Stepson

"I like how we can be a team Hazel Compton."

Dane steps from the shower and grabs a towel from the rung. He smiles to himself thinking of all he and Hazel have shared since yesterday. Something in him begins to stir deep inside, something he hasn't felt before. He turns to see her wrapped up in his sheets on his bed. He dries off looking at her and thinking how beauty, brains, and sexual chemistry beyond his wildest dreams just up and walked into his life...and he loves every minute with her! He walks quietly from the bathroom into his closet to get dressed. With the rest of the weekend off from the station he can concentrate on nurturing their relationship and giving her all the orgasms she desires. But first, breakfast.

Hazel has one leg draped over the side of the hammock with her big toe anchored to the porch floor assisting her leisurely sway. She looks up, watching the Spanish moss slowly flow from the trees surrounding Dane's property. The wind escapes through the strands of squiggly gray moss. She takes a deep breath to relax in a way that feels right in her soul. She thinks of him and feels fluttery inside. He's so very attractive both inside and out. She smiles remembering what they've shared so far.

She can smell the aromas he's creating in his kitchen. The smell of buttery biscuits mixes in the air with hickory smoked bacon and scrambled eggs. She smiles thinking of him and how sexy he looked standing in his kitchen in his boxer briefs after stripping down to hand her his shorts and shirt. He's a problems solver and offered up his outfit until she can find her romper. Without warning he literally gave her the shirt off his back and ordered her to the hammocks to rest. She smiles twirling a strand of her hair and thinking of ways she'll thank him.

"Now that's a smile I can look forward to." Dane is standing over her with a plate in each hand, no shirt on, and an apron tied around his slim waist.

She turns to see him in all his muscled wonder and can't help but giggle at his attire. The apron has "Kiss The Chef" written in cursive lettering on it. "Oh, I think I'm supposed to kiss the chef as instructed yes?"

Hazel reaches her slender fingers under the apron cloth and begins sliding her hand up. She likes teasing him. Dane purrs deep, his eyes closing slowly, "Come my little vixen, we need to eat or there'll be no energy for kissing."

She laughs out loud taking her hand back, "Okay, okay. Where do you want me?"

"Well, I can balance this plate on your tummy and pull-up a chair or…"

"No, no. I'll roll out of here and sit at your beautiful table there. We made such lovely dinner memories, I'm honored to have the opportunity to make breakfast ones...err, lunch?"

He smiles and pivots to place their plates down. "Coffee, juice,...both?"

"Oh uh, well I like both."

"Coming right up." Dane walks back to the screen door, his underwear showing his magnificent derrière from the back. She admires the v-shaped muscle structure to his back while taking a seat at the bistro table. He's prepared a culinary masterpiece, yet again. She feels she could get used to this.

A car pulls up and parks in front of Dane's house but on the street. Hazel sees it's an older Nissan and quite dusty. A female, in her mid-twenties exits and cautiously approaches the driveway. Hazel wonders if this stranger will ruin such a lovely day. Dane seems to be pretty popular, despite all his attention on her in the past weeks, he's probably got some interest from the town's female population or an ex or two floating about. Hazel decides to stay seated and hopes that the large envelope in the girl's hand is just a quick delivery.

Mandy Simpkey looks over and sees her seated at the table across from two huge hammocks. She smiles politely and walks down the long wrap around porch. Hazel begins to stand.

"Oh no, please don't get up. I'm just looking for Dane Hennie?"

Hazel smiles looking towards the screen door that opens. Dane bounds out with a pitcher of orange juice in one hand and coffee in the other. Although half-naked, he doesn't seem phased. Mandy's eyes quickly scan his body then she nervously looks over at Hazel.

"Hey Simpkey, everything all right?" Dane's voice is deep and smooth. The poor girl huffs nervously.

She raises the envelope, "Hi Mr. Hennie, I was asked to deliver this. Yes, everything's great...err you?"

Dane walks passed her and places the items on the table. He takes a moment to smile at Hazel and touch his finger under her chin before turning towards Mandy. He reaches for the envelope, "Oh okay. Good news I hope?" His eyes pierce down into Mandy's and she looks away and down at the floor.

Hazel notices how his energy affects the young girl. Although humid out, she seems to be slightly more vexed, beads of sweat forming at her temples.

"I'm not really sure. Mr. Clement asked me to drop it by after I delivered his groceries this morning...Merrill Clement."

Hazel's ears hear the name of the man her grandmother instructed her to write about. She looks up watching Dane carefully.

"Merrill huh? How's that old bastard doing?" He reads his name written on the front of the envelope then tosses the envelope onto a wicker chair. He places his large hands on his hips not caring how his bright red apron looks, or that it's tied around his boxer briefs in front of young Ms. Simpkey. He's very comfortable with his physique.

"Oh uh, well...he's still got that limp. Kruger is well!" Mandy tries to make small talk but fidgets with her keys looking uncomfortable at Hazel. She knows she's not from Melbye but she's seen her at the coffee shop in town on her laptop, then once with Dane. She thinks how life sucks now since the great Dane Hennie has a girlfriend. She can't wait to get in her car and tell the rest of the sorority group. They'll all be sad, especially when she tells them that he's with someone as gorgeous as he is.

Dane nods, "Well that's good to hear. I always liked Kruger."

Mandy looks at Hazel and smiles. Dane realizes Mandy isn't leaving. "Mandy Simpkey, meet Hazel Compton. Hazel, this is Mandy. She's in my nieces' sorority." He smirks knowing she'll go tell the town. Melbye is large but small-town gossipy. It annoys him.

"Hey." Mandy waves.

"Nice to meet you Mandy. Does Merrill Clement live far from here? Was it a long drive?" She looks over at Mandy's car which looks like it's been on a three day stretch through the desert. She also wonders how far she'll have to go to find Merrill. She had no idea Dane knew him. She's hoping he can help her.

"Nah, he's down off Kliveden a ways. He likes to stay out on his plantation so I take him his groceries."

Hazel smiles not wanting to eat in front of her, "Oh that's really nice."

Mandy takes the hint, "Well, I've got to get back. My shift doesn't end until four so."

Dane steps towards the porch entry lifting his hand to guide her but doesn't touch her, "Well, thank you for bringing that by Mandy. Please say hey to Dad for me will ya?"

"I sure will Mr. Hennie. A pleasure to meet you." She nods slightly to Hazel and turns to go.

Dane walks a few steps then watches her off. "Okay Mandy, bye now."

Hazel watches her leave then reaches for her bacon, she's starving and can't wait any longer. Dane turns to her, his eyes softening as he takes a seat across from her, "Ah finally, you and me and this beautiful day."

"It surely is. Thank you."

"Okay, dig in."

"This is amazing Dane. You are quite the cook! I may just have to follow what that apron commands." She chews, smirking up at him relieved their unexpected guest is leaving.

"Oh I hope you do Ms. Compton, I mean the apron says it so..."

"Hmmm...I think I've got some kisses I can share for my cook. Where'd you learn how to cook so well?"

Dane cuts into his food, "Well, my mother passed when I was nine so I kind of picked it up out of necessity. Dad worked twelve-hour shifts so I took care of my sister Gina and myself. But the real education into the culinary part started when I began hanging out at the fire station. I missed my Dad so I'd take my sister on my bike, and we'd hang out at the station with him. One thing about firemen, they have a lot of time, and it's a family! Big meals and even bigger stories is how life was...still is actually."

"I like that. I didn't have a big family. I've always wondered what that must be like."

Dane smiles looking deep into her eyes in the hopes that she'd someday want a big family, "Well, there's a lot of drama and self-sacrifice that happens with a family...but I wouldn't have it any other way."

She admires how altruistic he is. "So, what do you think is in that envelope?"

Dane looks over at the chair, "Oh that. I honestly have no idea."

"Aren't you curious?"

"Not really. Merrill Clement is an odd fucker. Not someone I have much respect for." Dane smiles chewing on a stripe of bacon. She enjoys watching his lips move as he chews. He's truly a handsome man who has no idea how sexy he is in the world.

Hazel chuckles at his blunt opinion. He knows how he feels. "Well, remember when I told you I moved here to find someone my grandmother made me promise to write about?"

"Yeah. I won't forget that day." He smiles taking a large bite.

She smiles knowing she won't forget meeting him either, "Well, that's who I'm supposed to find. Merrill Clement. My grandmother insisted I seek him out here in Melbye. I'm not entirely sure why."

"Hmmm...that's weird. Why would your grandmother want you to find an old college dean from South Carolina?"

Hazel stops chewing, "College dean?"

Dane nods, "Yup. I mean I don't know much about Merrill Clement other than he's from South Carolina, the father of my high school girlfriend, and err...a bit of a drunk."

"Do you know what college?"

"What?" Dean pushes his biscuit into his egg to try to pick it up.

Hazel has stopped eating wondering if Merrill Clement is the asshole dean that did nothing to help her when she reported her assault to the administration of Fenny College all those years back. She looks down, her eyes searching, she can't understand why her grandmother would do this. Why would she send her to Melbye if it involves all that?

"Do you know what college Mr. Clement was the dean of?"

"No. I don't know much more about him. Do you think he was a lover or someone important to your grandmother? Any thoughts as to why she wanted you to meet him...to write about him?"

Hazel tries to keep herself from speculating and overthinking too much about it, "Not just yet."

"Well, there's been gossip over the years but I don't know how much of it is true. I try not to entertain the drama kings and queens of Melbye."

"I get that. Could you share some things?"

Dane sits back putting his utensils down, "Ah, people are just cruel. It's been said that Merrill was such a mean drunk that his wife and daughter just up and left him. Took off to Vegas to start a new life there. Some dance company or something. That was years ago. No one's heard from them other than Wendy's brother, Merrill's stepson. Apparently he visits his mother and sister on occasion and says they want nothing to do with Merrill ever again."

"Oh."

"Yeah, not much else has come of it. Then again, I've stayed away from all that after Wendy left."

Hazel leans in, her elbows on the table, "Wendy was your ex?"

Dane nods, "Yeah. She was big into dance. In high school and all. She left with her mother and never spoke to me again. I was pretty busted up about it. I tried to find her but she very clearly did not want to be found. Then again, her brother isn't the greatest source of truth."

"Why?"

"He's just not a stand up guy. There's something off about him. I've never liked him...and he has a thing for young girls. I see him talking to the college girls at O'Tooleys and around town. It's odd. I don't know, I've never liked his manipulative nature. It's like he's a con but something tells me he's more sinister than that."

Hazel moves her food around her plate, "I can understand why you get an uneasy feeling."

Dane notices she's gotten quiet. Her smile has faded. "You feeling all right Haz? The food okay?"

"Oh yes, sorry. No, I love it!" She composes herself and pushes her thoughts aside.

Dane leans in, "Listen, I've got the rest of the weekend free. I was thinking, if you're up to it, I'd like to take you to a favorite town of mine about two hours away. Have you ever been to St. Ives?"

She finds her smile again. The look in his eyes is so sweet and wanting. "I have not. Why is it your favorite?"

"It's just a magnificent historical town with shops and restaurants, spas, hotels, museums, and seven fire stations around the city! I'd love to take you on a tour, maybe get massages, eat German food or Portuguese paella. Get a really nice suite with a hot tub..." His face looks innocent like a young boy. He's hoping she's up for some adventure with him.

"Well, I don't know sir, I just met you only a few weeks ago." She smiles teasingly.

He laughs, "Oh, you don't approve of my sleepovers?" He spreads his hand over their meal and then waves towards to the porch and house, finishing by pointing towards his back bedroom.

Hazel sits back against her seat, lifting the coffee cup to her mouth and smiling seductively, "Well, now that you've reminded me of how nice your hospitality is..."

"This was just the beginning Ms. Compton. An impromptu first date." He sips his coffee, mirroring her.

She feels she'd like to go and forget some of the things that began to stir in her mind learning about Merrill Clement and his evil stepson. "Well, I'll need to stop at my house and get an overnight bag but I think I could use an adventure. Might make for some neat paragraphs in a novel I'm trying to finish."

"Well then, why don't we get you showered. I'll clean up this mess." He wavers his eyebrows, teasing her now.

"How about I help you here...and you help me in the shower?"

"I like how we can be a team, Hazel Compton."

Chapter 16

Call out

"Nothing about this feels wrong."

C

huck Hennie walks around to the dispatch room and peaks his head in. "Hey lad, my son here yet?"

Ryan Leggue looks up at the monitors and sees Dane's truck isn't parked in the back lot. "No sir, not yet."

"Hmmm, no calls?"

"Not too much going on for a Saturday, might want to check with LT."

"Alrighty, thank you." Chuck frowns looking down at his cell. It's odd for Dane to be late and not check in, he smiles thinking about his son and his lovely new guest. He walks to the far end of the West hall and knocks on Lieutenant Patrick McCoy's door frame before stepping in. He waves Chuck in as he's finishing up a call. He hangs up and smiles at his friend. "Hey Chuckles, how goes it?"

"Hey Pat, doing good? How was your time off?" Chuck takes a seat in one of the chairs across from Pat's desk wondering why his office chairs aren't as comfortable.

Pat leans back, his chair creaking slightly, "You know, damn good. Got some time on the lake fishing, was able to relax, girlfriend blew me...wife blew me better."

Chuck laughs out loud feeling a bit guilty for doing so, "I don't know how you do it Pat."

"Well me either friend, or even why. What's more is one is my wife, the other's her sister!" Pat leans forward cackling and slapping his desk.

"Arsehole! I'm tellin' ya, I'm not covering fer ya if this turns into a scandal." Chuck juts a finger at him.

Pat laughs harder, "Old man, it's been over fifteen years now, that scandals been done and had. They're best friends and sisters, I'm just a pawn."

"Lucky bastard."

"That I am...that I am." He nods with a devilish grin. "So what's up?"

Chuck looks to his desk, "Just wondering if you heard from Dane?"

Pat looks down and rifles through some message slips, "Yeah, I was just getting through these, looks like your boy called out for his shift, switched with Jeremy actually. Doesn't look like he's back on until Monday evening into Tuesday."

"Huh."

"I can't complain Chuck. He's using a vacation day AND got his shift covered without me having to scramble so..."

"Aw nah, I know. He's a good boy. I just thought he'd want to go with me to Melbye Canal is all." Chuck smirks.

"Oh, what for that search with the rescue team?"

"Yeah, one of the young bucks thinks there's a vehicle down there stuck in the canal floor. Might be some more remains." Chuck starts to stand up.

Pat looks up at him, "They confirm that femur was human?"

"Oh it be human Patrick. It's nil wildlife."

"Hmmm, that's odd that Dane isn't all over it. He loves that kind of thing...and he's good at it too." Pat picks up his phone to start dialing.

Chuck looks back at him as he's leaving, "That he is. Got a new lady friend so..."

Pat lifts his eyebrows in surprise and smiles. Chuck waves and leaves his office. He thinks how his son wasn't too happy about him mentioning that the new recruit felt the vehicle at the bottom of Melbye Canal was a Volkswagen. He saw the pain in Dane's eyes again when he thought of Wendy. He realizes his son really doesn't want to be a part of the investigation. He thinks about it and puts himself in his shoes. He can't blame him. If that's her mother's car, and her body is in it, all these years he had thought she left him when she's actually been dead. He'll have a whole new guilt to go through. Dane usually deals with things in his own way. He seems to be more interested in healing with his new love interest.

Chuck heads out the back door to his truck. He wants to be there if that car is recovered from the canal. A bigger part of him hopes the recruit was wrong. Melbye would be turned on its' ear if Regina and Wendy Clement were found at the bottom of that canal. For eight years they've been in Vegas estranged from Merrill with Crosby Sills spewing lies. Chuck huffs as he starts the truck. *Oh shiet Melbye!*

■ ■

Dane walks behind Hazel and locks the door. Before shutting it he sees the envelope Mandy brought by. It's still on the wicker chair on the porch.

"I'll be just a moment." He leaves her for a second and walks the envelope back in the house then locks up carrying his overnight bag.

"You don't want to bring that?"

"Not at all, this weekend is about us and I'm on vacation. Whatever that is, can wait." He smiles and joins her at the walkway kissing her forehead. He has not a care in the world about the neighbors seeing him with her.

She smiles and leans into his soft lips. She loves them on her body. Dane escorts her to his truck and opens her door. She smiles, "I can walk to my house Dane, it's literally three houses down."

"I won't hear of it besides, that outfit should be illegal." He shuts the door and walks around to his side. She can see him laughing out loud.

She watches him climb up into the driver's side and squints evil eyes at him, "These are your clothes mister!" She giggles at his funny insult.

"I know. I know. The wedge sandals are a nice touch." He pokes fun at his baggy shorts and top she's had to wear since her clothes somehow found their way into his laundry basket. Dane doesn't mind, she's been mostly naked and he loves it.

Hazel reaches over to pinch his ribs but he hardly feels it. He laughs starting the engine. Before putting the truck in gear he looks over at her and sits back admiring her smile. He thinks she's so pretty and he loves that she's sitting in his vehicle and has finally slept over his house.

"What?"

"You look beautiful actually. I'm so happy we can spend this time together."

"Me too Dane. I'm enjoying every moment with you. Thank you, by the way." She smiles.

Leaning over he takes her cheek in his palm and kisses her. He stops and looks at her, "Is it wrong to want to make love to you already?"

"Nothing about this feels wrong. See my house over there? It has many rooms that need to be christened...if you think you're up to it."

He smiles kissing her again and puts the truck in gear to reverse out of the driveway. "I do love a challenge."

Chapter 17

Speechless

"Dane, I can't-"

D

ane and Hazel reach the touristy historic town of St. Ives by evening. It's only a two hour drive from Melbye but they spent a lot of time trying to pack an overnight bag and getting pleasantly distracted at her home. She's seeing the value of *not* rushing through moments.

Dane's truck rumbles through the narrow streets. People walk in and out of shops, breweries, bakeries, and many are getting on and off of the St. Ives trolleys. Hazel feels excitement with all the new sights and smells. She looks down watching Dane's gorgeous hand glide along her leg. His touch ignites her in between her legs and she finds she wants to mimic his caress with her own hand. She slides her slender palm across his thigh and inward towards the part of him that seems to be ready for her constantly. She can feel him getting firm as he smiles and looks forward at the cars in front.

"Jeeeezus, you're intoxicating Hazel. I thought fighting my body was rough all the times we were hanging out but now is proving to be much more complex. I feel like I'm going to have to pull over." He smiles, looking at her quickly.

She has a bedroom gaze in her eyes he's learning to recognize and a familiar ache begins deep within his groin. She smiles and whispers into his ear, "No need to pull over. You get us to the bed-n-breakfast and I'll just..."

He realizes she's not finished her sentence and is unzipping his fly. Before he can say anything her hand slides in warm and gently into his clothing. She works her way past his underwear and finds his manhood rock hard and wanting. She begins to caress him very slowly up and down his shaft, enticing him. Dan's breath hitches in his chest at the feel of her hand around him. He pulses beneath her palm, sexual desire and ache for her increasing.

Hazel snuggles closer whispering again, "Shame on you Dane Hennie, how could you keep such perfection from me all those weeks we were hanging out? So much pleasure hidden." She begins stroking inch by inch using his soft skin gently against his rigid length.

Dane bites his lower lip, his eyes blinking slow while watching the road. He loves how she treats him and finds he wants to be in her *again*. He begins to press on the brakes as he's approaching a light, "Well-" His words are gone as she leans down and places her mouth over the head of his penis. He looks around, shocked at her brazenness but loving the pleasure. The surprise is even more arousing. No one can see what she's doing due to the height of his truck. He sees everyone going about their activities.

Slowly and sultry like, Hazel moves down and then up, down again...then up. His breath slightly labored, Dane's mind feels blown with how pleasurable her mouth is on him. Hazel is extremely caring and precise with fellatio. The leisurely way she moves her tongue creates twice as much feeling.

MY HERO MY LOVE

The light turns green and he presses the pedal going a bit faster until he sees a back alley with no one. Hazel continues her slow assault on his rigid cock, loving how sizable he is in her mouth. She reaches her hand in and claps around the base of him to create more sensations. Dane pulls over and puts the truck in park. He locks the doors and rolls up the windows so the tinting hides them. He reaches to put the air conditioner on, his concentration slightly marred.

Hazel uses her free hand to slide up his chest and push his head gently back against the headrest. She wants him to relax and really enjoy how she suckles in between her tongue play along his shaft. He closes his eyes exhaling, her mouth is incredible! He feels he could erupt at any moment, his control now hers. Hazel pulls up letting her lips linger over every curve and muscle of his member. She loves the feel of him strong in her mouth but, she loves knowing he's feeling pleasure because of her. She tastes his precum and knows if she increases her rhythm he'll explode.

"Holy fuck...Hazel...you're-" Dane's hands come up, he runs them through her hair trying to hold off. He's getting close as she tortures him with her exquisite tongue. He brings his hands down and sweetly pulls her up. She lifts off him gently and follows his hold. Dane pulls her up and onto his lap, he reaches down and moves his seat all the way back. Hazel likes how strong he is but he never hurts her. His lips find hers hungrily. He reaches under her dress and caresses her vulva. She's moist with want for him. He pulls her panties to the side, then moves his hands onto her hips and slides herself down onto him as he burrows into her yoni. She's so wet and warm, her womb engulfing every inch of him. Hazel lets out a relieved moan at the glorious feel of him stretching and opening her. He feels so good inside her.

"Fuuuuuck-" She exhales, feeling how he presses against her clit. Hazel's head flies back and Dane reaches softly taking one of her breasts from the front of her dress and sinking his mouth down on her nipple. He pulls her waist with the other arm and begins rocking her on top of his lap. She moves in motion with the rhythm he sets and squeezes him inside each time he thrusts into her fully.

Dane presses up and in her, reaching all of her until he feels her most precious clitoris. He then retracts gradually, preparing to send waves of ecstasy through her once more. Hazel loves how considerate he is with her most sensitive areas and the sensations he sends through her make her want to cum over and over. She's never been so free and adventurous with anyone. He makes her feel like her true self in these moments, like she can finally breathe.

Dane releases his mouth from her other breast and tilts his head up to find her mouth. He thrusts up and she sinks down causing even more currents of satisfaction neither expected in the confined space of the truck. Her mouth is sweet and moist, he plunges his tongue in trying to breath her in. Hazel releases her mouth connecting her forehead to his as moans and breath exit her body.

She feels his hands slide up along her thighs to her ass as he seizes her firm cheeks with both palms and she likes how he pulls her down onto him rocking against her. Hazel feels the pressure, the pleasure, and all the sensations of excitement for being somewhat exposed in the vehicle. Her body starts to clench and she can no longer hold off from all that he's doing to her.

"Dane, I can't-"

He can feel her clench him inside and knows she's reached her end, she's given in to their union. He loves hearing her and allows himself to go with her. He pumps as she clenches. His seed spills inside of her pulsing and pulsing...feeling his heart ignite within their ecstasy...

Chapter 18

Runs Red

"I remember you now, Ms. Green Eyes."

T

he day has been long but just before sunset the car releases from the bottom of the canal as the crane bucks and lifts it up slow. Mud and water rush down the sides, as debris and vegetation sluffs off and splashes back down into the water. Everyone stares speechless as it is obvious there is a skeleton in pretty bad shape, strapped into the front passenger seatbelt. The driver side seatbelt is intact but the seat is empty. Chuck Hennie knows the car and contemplates texting his son before someone else does. The paint is faded and the convertible top is gone but it's clear it *was* a red Volkswagen bug. Everyone in Melbye knows only Regina Clement drove such a vehicle. Chuck hears his best friend dial his cell and speak to his dispatch requesting two on duty detectives from Melbye Police Department. He then mentions a second request.

Ron Dayton speaks calmly, "Rollins, I'm gonna need you to verify a vin number for me in a few but first, can you send patrol over to Merrill Clement's home to collect him and also his stepson, Crosby Sills. I want them both in separate interview rooms within the hour."

Chuck rubs his forehead looking down at his own phone. His son isn't picking up so he ends the call. He could text him.

He'll wait. He hopes Dane doesn't get any other calls about it. He wants to give him facts, not speculation which is what most of the people in Melbye spread.

■■

Crosby Sills lays on the cot and stares at the ceiling above. He takes a long drag of his cigarette and squints as his exhale burns one of his eyes just slightly. He sees her green eyes in his mind again, the hottie that Dane Hennie was sitting with at O'Tooleys all those weeks ago. He knows he's seen those eyes piercing at him before, it's driving him nuts he can't place her.

His phone beeps and he reaches for his cell lighting up the room showing a text. He pushes on the unknown number and sees the cryptic message:

the canal runs red with a bug

Crosby sees the message he was hoping would not come. Now he has to decide whether to stay hidden or head up north. There goes his job. Luckily he doesn't have to pay child support for Tommy anymore.

escort for MC and U on the way

Fuck. Crosby didn't think Melbye's finest would be so damn quick. If Merrill Clement tells them where his cabin is he knows he's fucked. He drags on his cigarette long and tries to think. He hates it up north, especially in the Carolinas or anywhere near Fenny College, despite the young girls. That could actually be nice and he has a buddy he could live with back in his old stomping grounds.

Suddenly, Crosby sits upright, he remembers! He speaks into the quiet room. "I remember you now Ms. Green Eyes. I remember your tight ass after I spiked your drink...You're the reason I got tossed out of Fenny by Clement and got into all this mess covering up his murders of my mother and sister. If it weren't for you opening your mouth, the mouth I should have spent some time in, I wouldn't be sitting here going through this bullshit...well, well, well, what a small world it is-".

Chapter 19

Naughty

"You are so welcome. I am enjoying you."

D

ane and Hazel walk into their bed-and-breakfast suite, the cool air hits them from the wall unit left on for their arrival. He places both bags on the floor then closes and locks the door. Stepping over their luggage he finds her waist and pulls her into his lips, he loves her mouth. She feels good beneath his hands, he likes how warm she is. Her smell is intoxicating.

She breaks the kiss, "Ohhhhh, how nice." She giggles as he walks her to the bed and lays her down along side of him.

"This is nice isn't it. I'm really happy you came with me. Not gonna lie, I a bit famished after our little side street detour." He smiles and she feels happy he's mentioning it. "Holy fuck Hazel, that was intense."

She wrinkles her nose at him, "That was kind of spectacular wasn't it?"

"You are lovely." He cups her face and kisses her again rolling her onto her back. He hopes she's as satiated as he is. He doesn't ever remember having so much sex in such a short amount of time, but their connection is divine to him.

She smiles and releases, "You are as well. That was fun and felt so...naughty-".

"That it did. I like your "naughty". It fits with mine." He looks at her amazed at who she really is underneath all her classic beauty.

She looks around the pretty, historically decorated room. It's nice that they have their own bathroom and she sees a sunken hot tub through the doorway and down inside the floor. "Oh wow, this is quite a suite, that sunken hot tub looks incredible."

He leans past her to see it, "It does. The internet pic doesn't do it justice. Look at those blue iridescent tiles."

"Right? What a great choice you made, Mr. Hennie."

He turns back to her smiling from the praise. His heart feels full as he notices he's not had this much fun in a long time. "Thank you. So tell me, are you wanting to stay in and order food or would you like to hit the town? We have all the way until one o'clock tomorrow before we have to be anywhere. I booked our couples massage downstairs for the afternoon just in case we need to sleep in."

"Oh, you are so on it aren't you? I'm loving how you take care of details."

Dane exhales, "I can be anal retentive about things...well, my father and sister tell me so."

Hazel laughs stroking his hair and running her fingers through it, "I don't see it as anal retentive. I actually enjoy you taking on the responsibilities. Thank you for this."

"You are so welcome. I am enjoying you."

"Same. Now, let's go out on the town so this dress sees more than the inside of your truck."

Dane pushes off the bed to stand and reaches to help her up. She steps close and presses into him, "It is a very nice dress and a very good idea for our truck fun."

■■

Dane places the menu down and checks his phone as Hazel decides what she's having. He sees two missed calls from his Dad and knows if it were three he'd have to call back immediately. He doesn't want to ruin this time with Hazel so he decides to just send a thumbs up emoji for his father. He'll call him Monday before work. He looks up and sees her smiling sweetly at him.

Her eyebrows furrow with concern, "Everything all right?"

"Oh yeah. Just checking in. My shift is covered, we're here enjoying St. Ives, and we have two and half more days. I am a happy man." He sips his beer watching her beautiful green eyes.

"I like that."

"I've been happy since I met you girl. You have some sort of *Hazel Magic*?"

"No, I think we just click, is all."

He smiles closing his eyes and nodding slow, "Oh my, do we ever."

She laughs at his dreamy reaction. He makes her feel really good about herself not to mention how good he makes her body feel. Her arousal starts to ignite again deep down inside. She's never been so attracted to anyone the way she is to Dane.

"So, did you always want to be a writer? I mean did you go to college for it?" Dane leans back his beer in hand, his eyes looking for their waiter, then back to her.

Hazel clears her throat, "Well, I had originally started out towards a journalism degree...but I don't do well with too much excitement or stress."

"Really? I think you're very adventurous."

Hazel exhales and smiles, "Well yeah, I mean I decided to stick closer to home and my grandmother instead of traveling all over. People and crowds aren't really my thing, but writing is."

He tilts his head slightly, "I wouldn't have thought that, you seem so cordial with people."

"I like some people, and I love writing about them...I just don't do well with strangers or too much energy."

Dane is intrigued, "How were you with college? Being around a college crowd was easier?"

"Not really. I think that's where I decided I was more of an introvert. I switched my major and then left school, completing my last year online."

The waiter comes over ready to take their order. Hazel orders first then sips her beer hoping she can change the subject. She doesn't want to think about college or why she left. Their romantic weekend is much more important to her than a past she can do nothing to change.

They both order and then Dane leans in placing his elbows on the table to be nearer to her. "So, where were we?"

"We were going on about college but what I really want to know is how you'd like to explore this lovely city! Look at the architecture of this place."

Dane looks around at the older colonial decor and dated building materials, "It's really neat isn't it? I think we should start with the trolley tomorrow, find some breakfast if we can, learn about the city for a bit, get our massages, and then we'll decide what else we'd like to do. There is a marina here if you're into a pirate ship tour or some dolphin sight-seeing."

"Oh, that sounds like so much fun!"

Dane likes seeing her face light up, "And after dinner, if you're up to it, they have these horse and buggy rides through the town at night. All the stores are lit up and it's really pretty to see."

Hazel sips her beer looking at him playfully, "That sounds lovely, let's do it. I wonder if the horse knows how to pull off down side roads or alleys." She winks at him giggling, reminding him of their little tryst in his truck earlier.

Dane puts his beer down careful not to swallow and choke. He loves how her mind works.

Chapter 20

Nothing
"Melbye Police Department."

T

wo patrol cars drive up and park in front of Merrill Clement's house. Three officers make their way up the porch steps, one turns right and makes her way to the side of porch to look in the windows and go around the back. The other two stand at the front door and one rings the doorbell, one knocks and announces "Melbye Police Department." Kruger begins barking but from a distance and sounds as if he is unable to come to the door.

The officers wait, one keys up his mic and gives an update, speaking into the radio clipped to his shoulder. The other reaches forward to ring the doorbell once more. Both are startled by an enormously loud crashing sound on the porch floorboards behind them! They jump while reaching for their weapons. The third officer runs around to meet them as all three stare down, guns half drawn, at a very dead Merril Clement, lying face-up, eyes open, his cane and one very bent leg beneath his body. They look up realizing he either jumped or was pushed from his second story balcony.

One officer keys up the radio to give dispatch another update and request the OIC on duty and an ambulance, the second opens the door and begins a search inside, the third bends down to check Merrill's pulse. *Nothing.*

■■

They begin kissing urgently, somewhat animalistic from the intense muscular and emotional massage releases and added hot tub fun. Dane grabs a hold of her jaw with his palm and begins to slow it down as he is a man who likes to take his time. Hazel loves it. His tongue is in her mouth sliding sweetly and unhurried. She presses her hips forward rubbing herself on his erection, tantalizing and arousing her clit in the rhythm of his breath. She then presses her breasts against his chest, her whole body feeling ready and sending him the message.

Hazel reaches down in the hot bubbly water and grips him just right. She can tell because he exhales a sensual moan into her wanting mouth. She begins brushing the length of his cock with her palm and considers going under water to take him orally. She hears another throaty moan escape him but then he moves his mouth to her neck, nibbling and suckling, causing her to lose thought. When he slides along and reaches her earlobe she feels ticklish shudders run down her spine and deeper into her inner erogenous zones.

Hazel pushes against his large chest causing him to back away. She lovingly guides him to stand and sit on the edge of the sunken hot tub. Dane looks sleepily down at her just in time to see her roll her mouth onto his tip then hollow her cheeks so she can slide all the way down to his base. His fingers find her hair and his head eases back. He sucks air in through clenched teeth as she sends ecstasy through him. All his thigh and stomach muscles tense and he knows he could spill into her mouth any minute. He's been aroused all day just being near her and exploring St. Ives along side her.

Dane picks her up under her arms and guides her to a stance. Once standing, she smiles the seductive grin he's learning to love. He moves her and then turns her away from him, sweetly bending her over the side of the hot tube having her place her breasts down and her face to the side. In a quick swoop he slides inside her from behind, causing her to mix a moan with a pleasing giggle. She clenches around him and he has to stop after the first thrust to compose himself knowing if he keeps moving he may end up giving in to her exquisite tightness and heat. He likes to exercise control until she's been satisfied but he's noticing the more comfortable they get with each other the more he wants to erupt sooner and sooner. He knows he's succumbing to her intoxicating energy and feels very deep emotion for her. Hazel drives him wild. He grasps onto her hips with both hands and spreads his legs wider to balance.

Hazel moans at the feel of his large hands on her. He sinks into her deeply but slow, just the way she likes it. She can feel so much more of him because of his patient, respectful style. He feels her contract against his head and shaft causing his breath to hitch again. The position, how she moves and moans, she knows she's sending him over the edge. Dane brings his hands in to grasp her tush and opens her ass to nuzzle further into her and the against soft mounds. Her hands reach out along the cold tile and he knows she's getting close. He slides his palm along her hip and then around to her front causing her to instinctively lift up letting his fingers into her softness to find her hooded wonder.

Hazel gasps and tries to speak, "You...you feel...so good..." but it comes out as an exasperated whisper into the echoing bathroom. Dane smiles, loving how easily she's pleased. She makes him feel proud of his abilities and their connection. His fingers continue to rub in a circular motion and her breathing becomes labored.

Hearing her, Dane can hold back no longer and plunges once again inside her, thrusting deep into her maddening warmth. Hazel moans loud, her body locking up as her breathing becomes a long drawn out moan. Knowing she's crashing into her tides of bliss he lets go too, spilling himself into her with quivering pumps of bliss, her exasperated breaths urging him on. They both fall into a heap of gratification allowing every body part and muscle to relax.

Catching her breath, Hazel finally begins to lift up, "Oh my gosh, I loved that. You're incredible. I'm exhausted...*in the best way.*"

"The touring, massage, food, and hot tub seemed to intensify things exponentially. I was worried I wouldn't hold out for you." He runs his palm down her spine as he lifts up, helping her to sit in his lap in the water.

Hazel nuzzles down into his chest as he wraps her up in his embrace. She smiles at how much fun he is to be with and how satisfying his love-making is. "I was having trouble holding out for *you*. I don't know what it is about you Dane Hennie but you rock my world."

"It's just the beginning Haz, it's *just the beginning...*"

Chapter 21

Things work out

"Hot damn Merrill, you actually did something right!"

C

rosby wakes up in a drunken stupor kicking over can's of Busch's beer while trying to stumble naked to the bathroom. He considers drinking more to get rid of his pounding head. His phone dings with a text he really doesn't want to check as it may be something about the cops not being able to find him or worse, something about Merrill Clement running his mouth before he can shut him up. He leans against the wall with one hand, the other on his hip while he leans over the bowl and pisses all over the floor. He couldn't care less as having a semi at his state feels more like a win. His phone dings again.

He slumps back into bed and reaches to read the message. It's from his contact at the station:

MC committed suicide. Jumped. They looking for you.

Crosby sits up trying to adjust his eyes as he cannot believe he's reading such luck! He was up drinking most of the night trying to figure out how to get rid of Merrill Clement before he snitched on them both out and now he can just let him take the fall.

"Hot damn Merrill, you actually did something right!" He shouts out into the cabin hearing his own voice and feeling less hung over all of a sudden. Crosby gets up and pulls on his shorts and a tank top. He steps into his work boots and grabs his keys. It's time to go a look for the green-eyed beauty he once knew and fucked twice. He can't forget her sweet face and he feels a celebration is in order. She started this whole mess and he feels she should be the conclusion too. This time though, he'll make sure she can't run and tattle.

■■

"How would you feel about staying an extra day?" Dane smiles mischievously and takes a bite of his bagel. He chews watching her eyes.

Hazel looks tired but peaceful. She swallows a gulp of coffee surprised at his question, "Dane Hennie, are you wanting to play hooky from your shift fine sir?"

"I'm really enjoying our time here. There's some more things I'd like to show you if you're up to it?"

"I do love it here, this town is just lovely. Truth be told though, I'm exhausted. I'm going to try to keep up but if I begin yawning while going in and out of the shops today just prop me up against a shelf and come back for me so I don't slow you down." She chuckles then yawns involuntarily.

He reaches and caresses her cheek with his fingers, "Tell you what, let's catch a show and sit and relax today. There's no hurry and all that hot tub action last night has got me feeling a bit winded as well."

Hazel loves how he listens. He's so different and she loves it, "Now you're speaking my language. I think I just need some recoup time."

"Well, I know of a great play two blocks over and then we can head back and take a nap. Who says you can't spend extra time in bed when vacationing."

"I would love that idea so much. I may even rustle up enough energy to reward you after that nap." She lowers her eyelids looking up at him with the gaze that makes his heart beat faster.

Dane doesn't say anything. He pushes her plate towards her to indicate she needs to finish her breakfast. She's fast becoming his favorite person.

Chapter 22

Vin number

"Got it. I've got to go. Talk later Dad."

Dane feels his phone vibrate in his pocket. Hazel is in the bathroom and they have twenty minutes before the play starts so he decides to see who it is. He has four missed calls from his father and the fifth is ringing. He answers despite telling himself he shouldn't.

"Hey Pops."

"Daney boy, listen...it's not looking good son. The VIN number on the vehicle, the Volkswagen...it's Regina Clement's car. I'm sorry, I didn't want to disturb you while you're away but it's going to be on the local news tonight. I didn't know where you are but was afraid you'd see it. I wanted to let you know Dane."

Dane's eyes close for a long moment, he leans back against the wall he's standing near. This is the exact reason he didn't want to answer the phone. The worst case scenario is realized. "All right."

Chuck Hennie hears his son go somber, he feels awful for him. "They're going to say a body has been recovered, well skeletal remains, and then the femur. There's no confirmation yet but they will mention the car belongs to Regina Clement who was last seen with her daughter Wendy eight years ago and presumed to be in Las Vegas. It's a mess son."

"That it is, Dad." Dane rubs his forehead. His guilt returns in his chest. All these years he thought Wendy left him after their fight about the baby when she most likely ended up in that car. He feels he should have looked for her instead of believing her liar of a brother and listening to him when he said she didn't ever want to hear from him again and that he picked her up from the abortion clinic before she took off. He remembers being so paralyzed with hurt he just shut the pain out.

Hazel steps out from the ladies room and looks left then right. She spots his gorgeous face and sexy, tall frame standing off to the side away from all the people. Her face shows concern when she sees him distressed and running his hand through his hair, his phone to his ear.

"And one last thing son and I'll leave you to the rest of your weekend."

"What's that, Pops?" Dane hopes his father has something positive to tell him so he can tuck the pain away behind it.

"Patrol went over to get Merrill Clement for questioning and he jumped from his balcony, committing suicide in front of them." Chuck says it as softly as the rest of his news.

Hazel walks up to him, coming close and into his side, he slides his arm around her, "Got it. I've got to go. Talk later Dad."

"Okay my boy, see you tomorrow."

"I love you."

"Love you too Dane. Be safe."

Hazel stares up at him. He's beautiful to her and she admires the bond he has with his father. She didn't have that with her parents because they passed when she was very young but she suddenly misses her grandmother. She waits.

Dane puts the phone back in his shorts pocket and turns looking down at her. He loves seeing her face. "Hey you."

"Everything all right with your father?"

"Yeah. There's some drama in Melbye he wanted me to know about before I hear it on the news."

Hazel's eyebrows raise in surprise. So far the town has been quiet, she was getting the impression it was going to be peaceful until she starting poking around for her grandmother. "Anything I can help with?"

"Naw, it'll be there Monday. I may need to get back and not stay the extra day." Dane's voice is low and he's not as happy.

"Would you feel better if we left now?"

"No, no I want to spend as much time with you as I can. Drama will always be abundant in Melbye. Let's see our play and take our nap, I can tell you all about it at dinner if you want." Dane kisses her forehead and smiles.

"Okay. Let's go be lazy and watch talented actors on stage." She wraps her arms around his torso loving how his large size and firm muscles feel beneath her hands.

"Exactly! We'll lay like broccoli and vegetate." He makes a joke and Hazel laughs out loud walking with him and feeling deep appreciation to be with him. Dane is so mild mannered even in the midst of drama and stress. She loves his demeanor.

Chapter 23

Not home

"It'll be there tomorrow."

C

rosby is careful not to be seen in crouched down in the little sedan he borrowed from his bosses tow lot. His hat is pulled down low, his long stringy hair pulled up in it. He sits hidden alongside of a shed on Nasrin Road adjacent to Renault Road where Hazel Compton rents Mrs. Yerro's house. His dispatch friend has proven to be quite an asset now that Crosby has made good on his promise not to repossess his car. He likes when he can call in favors.

He's been sitting on her house for three hours and Ms. Green-eyes hasn't left or turned on a light. It's getting dark and he's thinking she's not home. He was so looking forward to visiting her again and making sure she keeps her mouth shut...along with feeling her tight ass again but this time he's got his Sig Sauer. Just in case she wants to put up a fight. Crosby has no problems taking her out now that all of Melbye is focused on Merrill. He has an alibi of being out of town and with his old buddy so quick to lie for him, he'd never be fingered for any of the crimes. The police are too stupid and his inside contact has proven to be beneficial in the past. He's gotten away with so many in Melbye already and with Merrill gone, life is looking even better.

The conversation is getting uncomfortable but he wants Hazel to know about him before they get back to Melbye in the morning.

"She was carrying your baby?" Hazel stops chewing, feeling deep sadness for him. The look on his face is of sheer pain as he's been trying to explain a memory he obviously wanted to keep in the past.

"I'm not entirely sure. Her brother is a liar, always has been. He said we must have had a fight because she called him from the clinic and he picked her up. Shortly after, the same day, he said she and her mother took a vacation to Las Vegas to help her get over "things". We hadn't had enough time to discuss things. I had no confirmation, just confusing communication with her with no say in the decision which felt hopeless. I wanted a family! Honestly Hazel, my heart was so broken when I heard she left, I just poured everything I had into the fire academy and waited for her to call or return or...I couldn't believe she would do that to our child..."

Hazel reaches and cups his hand on the table. She knows she feels deeply for him because her heart feels as if it's breaking in two for the pain she sees in his eyes. She remains silent to give him the time to get it all out. She can see his eyes scanning the plate in front of him as he's articulating his feelings. For as much pain as he's endured, he's a very well adjusted man. No alcoholism, no drug use, no abusive reputation...just pure heartbreak. She wouldn't know what to do if someone made that kind of decision without considering her...then again, Crosby Sills made a decision to violate her without considering her even being a human being. She looks at Dane across from her, strong and masculine on the exterior, vulnerable and real on the inside. *God he's beautiful.*

She wishes she could take all his pain away. Fill the cracks in his heart with the liquid gold she feels he has inside him. As far as she can tell, it seems he's poured himself into his work and being a hero to keep going. She admires him even more for saving those children from that fire the first day she saw him. She feels so sad that he can save other's children but was unable to convince his girlfriend of five years to save theirs. Her eyes well up with tears for him but she doesn't move.

"Then the abandonment, it was all too much. And now, if that's her and her mother in that car. I mean if that's their remains, it means I didn't save her. I didn't even go look for her or try to find her on the internet. I just let it all go thinking I would just be a reminder of the life she didn't want here. It means I let her sit at the bottom of that canal all these years!"

Hazel nods, squeezing his hand. He tries to eat but returns his fork to the table. She raises her hand for the waiter and he bee-lines over to their table.

Dane continues, "And Merrill Clement, he's dead now, probably the only other person with answers...."

The waiter smiles. Hazel points to both their meals and speaks half-whispering, *"Could we get this to go and the check please?"* The waiter sees there is a situation, nods and scurries off. Hazel caresses his hand, Dane reaches for his wallet. He does want to leave and get away from being around so many people. She turns her focus to him again.

"I thought I was past all this but the thought of her being at the bottom of the canal all these years when I was told she was off happily married and dancing on stage like she loved...well, it just feels terrible." He leans back against his chair. Dane sees the tears in her eyes for him. He knows now he's in love with her.

Hazel's eyes are so sad, "It does feel terrible, Dane. It's one thing to feel as if someone has moved on and things just didn't work out. It's another to feel you've been manipulated and lied to for so long."

He nods, pulling cash out and putting it on the check. Hazel moves quickly to put their meals in the to-go containers. She wipes her eyes hoping no one sees. Dane sees and reaches to help her bag the containers. He stands then stepping around to pull out her chair and escort her from the restaurant. He feels awful that they showered and got dressed after their nap, just to have their evening ruined with sad news and rush through dinner. He wants to apologize.

"Hazel, my apologies for making things uncomfortable in there and cutting dinner short. I-"

She pivots and comes in close to him outside the restaurant doors, "Hey. Don't you apologize for feeling. I just got our food to go in case you needed to continue talking on this in a more private setting. This isn't easy Dane. I don't feel you deserved to lose your lover and your baby all in one moment, just to find out eight years later she may not have been leaving you at all! I know if I was her, I sure wouldn't have."

He looks down into her watery eyes, she's so kind and genuine. He loves her voice...her body, everything she is. Dropping the take out bag on the sidewalk he slides both hands under her ears cupping her face and bringing her lips to his. Dane kisses her deeply and with conviction. His mouth fevered and his tongue sweet, he plunges into her wanting mouth and she kisses him as much as he her. His lips feel slightly desperate as he desires her connection and wants to let her know how much he appreciates her. She's supportive without even trying to be, just pure nature and goodness. As much as he's hurting his heart is pounding in his chest for her. He feels her mouth wanting him and her hands slide around his body and onto his back. Her palms are warm, her touch healing. He moves his arms around her and pulls her deeper into his mouth. As close as they are, he wants to be closer. He wants to meld with her, escaping the hurt. Hazel is the best thing that's ever happened to him and he knows that now.

He pulls away, feeling arousal peaking, "Thank you for saying that, Hazel."

Hazel sits on the edge of the bed and bends down unfastening the strap on her heel, "Right, and you know Dane, it's somewhat strange that Merrill Clement had Mandy deliver that envelope to you don't you think? And then kills himself the next day? It could be a confession."

Dane stares at her from across the room. He'd not thought about that. He looks at her, she's beautiful the way she bends, her long legs shimmering beneath her dress, sun-kissed from their time in St. Ives.

"I hadn't thought of that Hazel. You may be right. I mean I don't really know him but he was the father of my ex-girlfriend. I thought it odd that he would send me anything after all these years. I was too excited to bring you here, I forgot all about Mandy delivering that from Merrill."

"Do you think you may want to head back and open it?"

He looks at her. She's willing to cut everything short for him. He doesn't want their night to end with a long drive home to Melbye. "It'll be there tomorrow."

She lifts her gaze to him. He looks remarkable sitting slumped down in the corner chair, his shirt unbuttoned and his dress pants snug in all the right areas. His tie hangs loose around his neck. He has one hand under his chin as he stares out the window, the other holding the whiskey and ice she made for him. He's distraught by everything he's been forced to think about since his father called.

"That's true." Hazel stands bringing her arms around her body and she lifts her dress up and over her head, letting it fall to the floor.

Dane sees the swift motion out of his peripheral vision and turns to see her. His eyes affix to hers then move down to her neck, her breasts spilling out from the top of her bra, then down to her panties and legs that end only when she steps out of her strappy heels. She's a goddess to him. She catches his gaze and watches him stare while his glass finds his lips. His eyes have gone from sadness to desire. She wants to please him, give him a break from all the stress that's visited them today.

Hazel feels a yearning for him. She sashays to him, her eyes lowering in the bedroom gaze that makes him come undone. He watches her above him, her hand reaching out to caress his face. His eyes close at her touch, the smell of her intoxicating.

He opens his eyes locking on her gaze again, he can feel his breath hitching and his cock growing. Just the feel of her energy near him ignites his every cell. Hazel places her hands on his thighs, her breasts hanging near his face. She thinks about leaning in to kiss him but decides to spread his legs and lean down to her knees. She watches his eyes and he watches her reach in to unfasten his slacks. She smiles at him and finds what she's after without looking away from his gaze.

Reaching in, she finds what she wants and frees him. Dane watches her mouth so close, he can feel her warm breath. She's so gentle, she clasps him in her palm and his eyes close at the pleasure of her touch. When he opens his eyes he sees her mouth sweetly engulf his head, her tongue searching for his precum. She swirls her tongue, then in one swift move she pulls his dick forward and deeper into her throat. He reacts with a deep inhale, the world feeling safe again...he deep within her soft, loving mouth.

Hazel begins her caressing moves along his shaft her other hand coming in to cradle his scrotum. Dane finds the shelf with his glass, leaving it so he can run his fingers in her long hair. He watches her going down and then up on his most sensitive area. He feels aching deep within as she taunts and tantalizes every nerve ending in the most enjoyable way. His breathing is erratic as he tries to maintain control. He watches her more, her cheeks hollowing, his penis deep within her loving mouth. She drives him wild, helping him forget everything else.

With Hazel, she makes it divinely personal, he loves that about her and how she's so connected to him. She's the kind of woman that only understands how to touch lovingly. It's her nature, and he wants it, he loves her nature.

Hazel releases somewhat, spending some time swirling and suckling her tongue around his rim. The feeling is exquisite, a moan escaping him. Hazel smiles and exhales slow, loving how he enjoys her. She begins to take him in again deep but feels his hands softly cup her face. He gently lifts her off him and brings his mouth into hers, kissing her fiercely. She accepts him and feels how intense and aroused she's made him. Dane lifts her up standing abruptly to press against her body. His mouth hungry for her, his body more so. He backs her up until her legs stop at the end of the bed. Reaching down he grabs one leg under her knee and lifts it high on his hip causing them both to sink down into the large bed. Dane straddles her and moves his engorged cock into her, her panties preventing what they both want.

Hazel pulls at his slacks and underwear just enough to lower them, she lifts her legs up higher opening herself enough for Dane to feel her underwear is crotchless. He smiles into her mouth and she pulls at his waist. She wants him deep within her as she is now soaked with desire for him. He ignites every cell in her being.

Dane does as she pleases and slides hardness long and into her. He buries into her warmth and delights in how she cries out thankfully into the air of their room. Hazel squeezes him tight and releases so he will thrust again and deeper. Breath escapes him as he slides into her heated, wanting womb.

She brings her legs up around him, her tongue searching his mouth, her hands pulling him into her. Hazel feels a familiar sensation erupting inside her as she clenches and cradles him inside her. He arouses all of her and she feels she's losing control faster this time as they've shared so much emotion.

Suddenly, light tremors of sensation begin to tingle at her clitoris and then down and inside, her breathing quickening. Dane picks up their rhythm knowing she's close by her breathing and nails digging slightly into his skin. It's beyond stimulating and he stays with her, thrusting and building into rumbles of pleasure. His mouth comes crashing down onto hers, their tongues intertwining leading them both into to an electricity and then an explosion that hits them like a storm, making them shudder and dive into their bliss together...

Chapter 24
Union
"Well, well, well..."

A

s the afternoon begins, the sun highest overhead, Dane sits down in his hammock not quite wanting to know what's in the envelope he holds in his hands. He doesn't want to know more that could ruin how well his life is going with Hazel. Then again, he wants to know everything to work through all the uncertainty. He looks over and down the street at her house.

He smiles seeing the light on through the window of her bedroom. He misses her already and all the things they've shared with each other. He sees her walked past the window and butterflies swirl within. She's his person. He knows it now because he aches even when she's just down the street in her home away from him.

Dane exhales hearing his phone vibrating on the porch floor below the hammock. He knows he needs to head into the station or at least touch base with his father...he just doesn't want to deal with so many old memories. He looks at the envelope again, his name scribbled on the front in such a haphazard style, like a doctor scribbling a prescription. He takes another deep breath and unfastens the clasp. Inside there appears to be a chunk of paper. He pulls it out reading the first line:

MY HERO MY LOVE

To Dane Hennie,
Because of my selfishness, my unhealed parts-
I killed them...

■ ■

Hazel steps out of the shower and before the window steams up she looks through it and over towards Dane's house. She sees him. He looks so serious sitting in his hammock reading. Admittedly, she's curious about the contents in Merrill Clement's envelope. She thinks of her grandmother and the promise she made to come to Melbye and seek out Clement. Her grandmother did not mention why or that Melbye was such a small town. She smiles at how she met Dane and that he's the ex of Clement's daughter. Her smile fades as she remembers how his stepson is Crosby Sills. *Damn small town for sure.*

She cants her head, seeing him slowly disappear behind the fog on the window, his large frame stretched out, his forearm resting atop his head as he reads on and on. She looks in the mirror deciding she'd rather stay in and cook him dinner than get dressed and go out. Knowing he's probably reading something very intense involving Wendy and her now dead father, she's thinking he may need a quiet night in for himself. She already misses him. She knows Dane is a strong, caring soul but the strong, caring types also need time. She knows she wants to be there for him and deep down hopes he still comes over.

She dries off, tousling her hair so it dries curly. Stepping back she gazes at her nakedness in the mirror feeling quite confident. Dane makes her feel things she's never experienced before. She smiles, running her fingers down her neck and across her clavicle. Her body remembers the feel of his lips on her skin, his hands caressing her breasts down to her tummy and beyond. It reacts with a quiver inside at the memory of him entering her as she opens to his want for her. Their union has become something she yearns for, hour by hour, and she's quite surprised at how she longs for him more now that he isn't near. She's never felt this way towards a man. He is quite special. Her heartbeat quickens in her chest.

A thump resounds from out in the house and she smiles realizing he must have walked swiftly to her front door. Quickly, she rushes to her bureau to pull on shorts and a tee shirt. It's not exactly what he'll be expecting since they were supposed to grab some dinner at O'Toole's, she smiles thinking he'll be pleasantly surprised and probably relieved.

She hurriedly pulls on the clothes, fixes her hair once more in the mirror, and slams the drawer shut. She steps into her flip flops and reaches for the doorknob. As soon as she opens the door to rush to him Hazel find herself face to face with the worst human she's ever encountered in her life...and a gun pointed right at her throat!

"Well, well, well..."

Chapter 25

Shrill

"Dane, sit down son. I know you're upset but we have to figure this out."

D

ane sees his father's truck slow down in front of his house and pull to the curb to park. He loves his father deeply, but he sure as hell doesn't need a conversation about Melbye drama right now. Reading Merril Clement's confession letter has brought on about the worst emotions he could experience after such a wonderful weekend away. He feels his temper brewing.

He's been trying to get it under control but has half a mind to go smoke Crosby Sills out of that hidden cabin in the swamp he thinks no one knows about. Merril confirmed thats where Sills will be hiding but Dane's known about that old broken down cabin since high school when he and Wendy lost their virginity in it. Crosby isn't just a twisted rapist, Dane knows he's stupid as well.

He watches his father limp from his truck and up to him on the porch. His face full of sadness for his son. Dane's made it to the farthest chair, trying to muster energy to go and take Hazel to dinner as he promised. He knows he loves her with everything in him. Especially now, knowing what Crosby Sills did to her in college and how Merrill covered it up to protect the reputation of his family and that of Fenny College. He hurts knowing now why her grandmother wanted her to come to Melbye. He hurts also knowing how she must be feeling keeping such a shameful secret with her rapist walking around free.

And how confused she must be knowing now that the man her grandmother asked her to interview is dead. He fears the closure her grandmother wanted for her won't really be closure at all, now that he's got the answers in the confession letter.

The pain of all that's in this town could make her leave. He swallows knowing that the absolute love of his life, only a few doors down, could abandon him just as the first love of his life did.

"You alright' lad?" His father touches his face then grunts sitting down in the wicker chair across from him. Chuck Hennie feels heartbroken for what he has to tell his son and how he has to persuade him to go to the police station to be interviewed.

Dane has the large envelope on his lap, his hands clasped, his chin resting on them. He leans forward placing his fingers together and resting his elbows on his knees. He looks from his father down to the floor, fury seething within.

"Pops, you know how when you're in a fight with fire and the beast is coming...you're there and..."

His father moves, mimicking his posture. He leans forward with his eyes on his son. He's the most gentle but fierce creature he's ever met. He remembers thinking it when he first held him in his arms. There is no better man.

"...how it feels like the end, it feels like every cell in your body has tried. You've fought for hours and you just make the choice to let it consume you if you have to but..." Dane pauses, trying to keep his anger under control.

Chuck reaches for his son's hand and places his on it. He knows exactly the fight Dane is struggling with inside. Dane is a man's man and his heart is breaking for him. He's at war within himself. He knows he'll choose right now and he wants to believe he chose right with Wendy.

"...but you give it just an inch, a moment more...because you can't let the demon win. You can't let hell take you?"

Chuck nods, a tear falling from his cheek to his forearm for his boy. He must have loved Wendy so deeply that the memory haunts him like *hell*. He hates to have to tell him he's got to go in to be interviewed as a possible suspect to Wendy and her mother's murders. A boyfriend or spouse is always a suspect and must be ruled out. Dayton granted him one request, that he be the one to go get his son and bring him to the station for questioning.

"It's going to be okay, my boy."

Dane's eyes raise to his fathers. He sees his pain too, but he's way past that. He's almost shaking with rage.

"Whatever comes of all this, I know you loved her."

Dane frowns, "Who? Wha- Wendy?"

Chuck nods seeing his son's face change to confusion.

"Pop, that was years ago. I was young...and stupid. She made me believe she was capable of killing our baby, but it wasn't mine."

Chuck sits back against his chair unable to understand what he's hearing. He only heard about their breakup, not that there was a pregnancy. His chest aches knowing his son may be confessing to motive. He wonders if he should stop him.

Dane picks up the envelope and hands it across to his father, "It's all right here. Merrill Clement read her journals. Fucking Crosby, that rat-bastard-mother-fucker was the father! He forced her to breakup with me, he forced her to get an abortion because the child was his. She didn't stop loving me. She didn't kill our baby and run off. Her fucking drunk of a father killed her and his wife in the car and called Crosby to come take care of the mess. Crosby dumped his mother and sister at the bottom of Melbye Canal to cover up *his* crime

AND save Merrill so he wouldn't go down either. The two hated each other because they had dirt on each other, not because Wendy and Regina left them. Merrill realized the gig was up Dad, he killed himself as a justified sacrifice and to let Crosby Sills finally take the fall. It all started with fuckin' Crosby! The guy is a cancer."

Chuck sees spit fly from his son's mouth as he speaks the man's name. He brings his hand up to his mouth shocked at the pain his son unknowingly had to endure. He understands his rage now. All these years he thought he was to blame. All this time he hurt over losing his own baby...that wasn't even his!

Dane huffs, a smile of indignation appearing for just a moment. "Oh, and here's the real kicker Dad, you're gonna love this fucking serendipity. The woman that moved here, to write a book about Merrill Clement as per a promise she made to her grandmother on her deathbed...Hazel? The woman I've fallen madly in love with...has no idea that her grandmother's private investigator found out why the fucking dean of Fenny College covered up her rape there..."

"Wait son, what?"

Dean stands and starts rubbing his forehead, then pacing, he hates sharing Hazel's private torment but knows it's all going to come out because of Clement's twenty-three page admission. He's trying to think of how he's going to explain the confession letter to Hazel. How she's going to be exposed because Crosby Sills is a roofie abusing rapist predator. He runs his hand through his hair realizing how many times he's seen Crosby around the young college girls...even his niece! He inhales and continues.

"Hazel Compton moved here at the urging...err deathbed promise to her grandmother that she would come to Melbye and find and write a novel about Merrill Clement. Hazel didn't know why, but kept her promise to her grandmother and look...look Dad, she's right there...with all this unknown pain waiting for her. And she's...she's so beautiful Pops, like inside and out and just full of goodness-" Dane shoves his hand towards her house.

Chuck looks over to the cute little Yerro house, "She doesn't know Merrill?"

"She doesn't know why she's here. I mean now she really doesn't know what she's going to do since the guy her grandmother wanted her to meet is now fucking dead. She's obviously been trying to keep her secret hidden and probably terrified to run into Crosby! She's confused and I'm sure looking for reason. She knows this piece-of-shit has given me this...whatever, death confession here. She hasn't read it but she's going to ask me. Hell, I'm supposed to be over there right now picking her up for dinner Dad. What am I supposed to say? Oh hey babe, I know all about your college rape that was covered up by your rapist's stepfather, who by the way knew his stepson fathered a child with his own daughter, forced her to abort it, and oh yeah, covered up her car accident, caused by his drunk ass, and didn't know by his ass-wipe of a stepson dumping her and her mother's body in Melbye Canal that it would come back to haunt him years later...but hey, let's go to dinner babe..." He juts his hands down at his side furious, his sarcasm rare.

"Dane, sit down son. I know you're upset but we have to figure this out."

Dane looks down at his father, "I don't want to sit down Pop! I want to go burn down that fucking shit-hole cabin with Crosby in it, a hole from my shotgun blown straight through his black heart!"

Chuck stands trying to calm him. He places a hand on his shoulder to stop him from raising his voice and pacing. "Son please, I was sent here to bring you into the detectives at Melbye PD for a statement."

"What!?" Dane looks into his father's eyes unable to believe what he's hearing. He knows being Wendy's boyfriend back then and her body being recovered he's going to be questioned.

"Lad, you need to bring that envelope and come with me. Merrill Clement is a feckin' manky dosser and Crosby...well, we need to find that piece of..."

A gunshot resounds through the neighborhood, then a shrill scream comes from Hazel's house. The sound a woman should never have to make. Dane's head averts from his father to her house. He runs down the porch and heaves his body over the railing, his legs moving quickly straight for her home. Chuck rushes to his truck to call for help and drive to her house to help his son.

Chapter 26
Saved me

"I did save you...because you saved me too. I love you-"

"

Shut your dick hole, you bitch! If you'd kept your mouth shut back at Fenny none of this would be happening. Yeah, you thought I wouldn't remember those eyes right? Or that tight ass when I saw you at O'Toole's with Hennie? Bet you thought you could just come live here in my town with all your righteous bullshit...like you could forget me and put it all behind you. Tell me Ms. Compton, did you justify the drugs you had in your system at that party?" Crosby spews the question at her through clenched teeth, his gun pointed at her, his other hand undoing his belt and fly.

"Fuck you. I'd never done a drug in my life. You roofied my drink you pencil-dick rapist!" Hazel backs away as her words anger him. Blood trickles from her bottom left lip, her tank top ripped almost exposing her full breast. She scans the room trying to find a weapon to hit him with or hit the gun in his hand. She knows a coward like him only feels power with a gun pointed at his victim...or when they're unconscious and can't fight. She's going to fight him this time even if it means taking a bullet.

Crosby wipes his mouth on his arm, the blood from his nose trickling down to his lips. Surprisingly she's got fire in her and broke his nose the second he lunged at her. If he could see clearer he wouldn't have lost the grasp he had on her but the sting of his nose let her slip free and she's run into the living room away from the bed he so wanted to use. Now he's got her pinned near the door like a rabid animal backed into a corner.

"Oh, pencil-dick is it? Bet you didn't think my dick was so small when you woke up and felt what it did to you. Tell me, did your faithful friends ever come looking for you...or did the fraternity guys find you?"

Hazel narrows her eyes, she hates him to her core. She calms her breathing and lowers her voice, "Oh yeah, you're a real big man Sills. Can't get anyone to sleep with you so you go around drugging college girls. I bet you have an affinity for fucking the dead too...since you like your victims unconscious and not able to tell you *HOW BAD YOU ARE WITH YOUR MIDGET DICK*!"

"Fuck you, bitch!" Crosby aims and squeezes the trigger he said he wasn't going to for fear the neighbors might hear. He wanted to have her one more time before making sure she'd never talk. His temper takes over and the gun blazes!

Hazel is quicker than he thought and falls to the floor, the bullet missing her and shattering the mirror that was on the wall behind her instead. She lunges forward, determined to grab the gun or his pants hoping to drag either down enough to catch him off balance. With all her strength she punches him as hard as she can in the very area he assaulted her. If she had a knife she would have sunk it into his groin to make sure even in prison he couldn't hurt another human.

Crosby heaves forward in pain, the gun dropping from his hand, the pain in his dick and balls searing like burning fire throughout his body.

"Ahhhh, you whor-" His words cut short by his need to take his anger out on her. Before she can reach the weapon he grabs her by the throat and squeezes, trying to crush everything that makes her words formulate. Hazel swings both her arms making sure to scratch him violently on the face, the right side then the left. He squeezes harder slamming her up and down onto the couch he plans to use if he can turn her over. He much prefers women with their backs to him when he takes what he wants.

Hazel swings wildly once more fighting for her life. She decides if he's going to take a piece of her again, this time she'll fight him to her last breath. He pushes an elbow out blocking her one arm, she swings wild and fast with the other again aiming for his eye. It works! Crosby screams, his eye sliced by her nail.

He jumps back, determining he needs the gun to get rid of her. He crouches down, one palm over his eye, the other reaching for the gun just as the front door is kicked in, the frame shredded. The door slams against the wall as Dane's body heaves into the room. He sees Crosby near his feet and then Hazel bloody, her clothes ripped, one breast almost exposed.

Rage and instinct consume him, instead of grabbing the gun, he grabs Crosby by the hair and belt buckle and picks him up. The gun goes off again, nearly missing Dane's leg while the bullet lodges into the wall. A growl of fury from years of pain and manipulation erupts from Dane and he heaves Crosby's entire body up and through the large front window, shattering it into pieces. Crosby screams landing out on the grass and at the foot of Dane's father who's armed with only a fire ax and Irish curse words telling him he better not move!

Dane runs to Hazel and she wraps her arms around him, "Baby? Baby, Hazel? Are you hurt? Baby? I- I love you, are you hurt?"

Hazel hears him despite the pounding in her ears, she hears his voice, the voice she's learned to live for over the past month. He's breathing erratically, she as well. His chest rises and falls, adrenaline coursing through him. His touch gentle. She can't speak, she squeezes him around his neck never wanting to let go.

Dane releases from her death-grip to look her over. Frantically he pushes her hair out of the way and pulls her shirt to cover her breast. He checks her body and her face, "Are you hurt, is anything..."

"I-"

He sees she's banged up but alert. He kisses her forehead, "Oh sweetie, I'm so, so sorry. I'm-" He can't find the words. What do you say to someone who's been raped, pushed aside, forgotten, and then assaulted again by the same monster. He kisses her cheeks, her forehead, "Hazel, I-"

"I...love you too." She finds the whisper to say to him, the words only meant for him. "you...saved me...you...my...*hero*-." She grabs him close and sinks her face into his neck. He picks her up and walks her out the door to get her away from the scene and into his truck to take her to the hospital. She keeps her face hidden in his neck where it feels safe and he smells so good. He feels so safe...

Dane looks over and sees his father glaring down at Crosby. Chuck looks up at his son and relaxes his ax letting it hang from his hand. Dane stops looking from his father to Crosby watching him take his last breath with a huge piece of glass impaled through his torso, another through his right thigh severing most of the leg. Crosby Sills' face falls to the side, his eyes open. Dead.

Chuck looks at Hazel limp in Dane's arms and looks back at Crosby like the piece of shit he is. Neither of them attempt to resuscitate him. Neither even try. It goes against their code of ethics but not their deeper code as father and son.

Chuck nods to his son and Dane nods back. He looks to his truck urging his son to take her in it to the hospital. Dane steps with her away from the man he just killed. He begins approaching the passenger side of Station #6's rig. Neighbors begin to walk over and are staring. Sirens blare at the end of the street and get closer. Flashing lights become brighter and disturb the beauty of the their little neighborhood. He opens the passenger door and places her down gently. She whimpers and clings to him harder not wanting to let go of him. Her body is rigid and scared. Her breathing is erratic and it breaks his heart to feel her desperation at not wanting him to release.

The sirens engulf them as an ambulance and other emergency vehicles arrive. Officers drive up and onto the lawn, doors open and slam, dispatch can be heard over the radios, commands are given. Dane stays with her, holding her as close as she needs. He buries his face in her hair just wanting it to be the two of them. Wanting her to be okay and not injured.

"Hennie, she need an ambulance?" Dayton's voice is soft as he speaks to Dane not wanting to disrupt them more than they have been. Dane nods.

Chief Dayton looks over at the EMS guys, "She's over here."

Dane picks her up into his arms, "I'll take her to the rig. My pops is with the other victim. He's DOA." His voice is deep, she whimpers hearing him so close. She can't feel her body, but she can feel his around her somehow. He's all she wants.

He walks her over and up into the ambulance placing her down on the gurney. She won't let go, her eyes closed and pressed into the nape of his neck. "Shut those doors will ya Benny?"

Dane tries to get her some privacy from all the sounds and the glares of prying eyes. Hazel is half-clothed and still wrapped in his arms. He tries to ease her as he's crouched down along side of the gurney he's placed her on. He has enough training to evaluate her and assess if she needs to be taken in. "I'm not going anywhere. I'm just going to loosen my hold so we can put a blanket around you baby. Can you let me do that Hazel?"

She doesn't respond and only nuzzles in closer to him trying to move off the gurney. Dane looks over at Benny, his EMT friend of nine years. "Could you give us a moment bud...and lower those lights for a bit?"

Benny nods, doing as he asked and leaves out of the side door. Dane can hear the arrival of the big fire truck and the sirens cut off. There's no fire but as soon as everyone heard the call involved him and his father, everyone hit lights and sirens to show up. He just wants to be with Hazel. He'll wait all night if that's what it takes for her to let go of him.

Her breathing begins to slow just a bit. She's taking longer, deeper inhales and exhales. She wants to cry but there's still too much adrenaline rushing through her veins. All she can do is try to feel him close as her body trembles in fight-or-flight reaction. Her eyes are closed frantically moving back and forth as she tries to reconcile everything that just happened. Dane reaches to caress her hair. He cradles her and kisses her forehead. He's so grateful she wasn't shot or bleeding anywhere.

"Is- *Is he...dead?*" She whispers to him and he's so happy to hear her try to speak. He nods in response, distraught that he just took a life but relieved it resulted in her being in his arms.

Hazel can't believe it. She wants to know the monster is finally gone, she leans away and looks him in the eyes, blood all over her mouth, a large bruise forming. "Is he dead, Dane?"

Dane sees her beautiful face begging to know, her mind trying to reconcile that the man who hurt her all those years ago has finally gotten what he deserved. He looks at her whole face, pushing her hair away from her mesmerizing green eyes he loves so much, "Yes baby, Crosby Sills can never hurt you again. I promise Hazel. He's dead and you will never have to see him again."

"You saved me Dane." She whispers it, her eyes searching back and forth in his. "*You*...saved me."

Her voice cracks as emotion overwhelms her. Her eyes furrow and tears begin to form as she begins to accept the words he said about never being hurt again. He feels so bad for her, his heart aching. He kisses her gently so as not to cause pain. He wants her to know he did save her, and he'd do it a hundred times over because that's what is needed. A man should save a woman, not take from her.

"I'll always save you Hazel. That's what should have happened for you all those years ago. I'm here and I'm not going anywhere." He moves his hands to cup her face and look deeply at her, "I did save you...because you saved me too. I love you-"

Tears fall from her eyes as she realizes he knows. She looks at his lips saying the very words she's needed her whole life. He did save her...he saved her with his hero heart.

Chapter 27

US

"Yes, us my hero...us."

H

azel locks the front door and walks down the hall towards their room. Dane is stretched out on the bed reading in black boxer briefs which she absolutely loves on him. He reaches to turn a page and she watches the muscles of his bicep ripple beneath his gorgeous skin. It's been six months since she moved in with him and she's not regretted it once. He went through remorse for taking a life, she went through the trauma her body required but, since that night they've not been a part and she's never been happier. Once a week they go for counseling together to make sure Crosby Sills is no longer the connection between them. She didn't think she could love Dane more but each day proves her wrong.

She watches him, his eyes moving along each sentence, his gorgeous face glowing in the low romantic light of their bedroom. She runs her finger inside the silk belt of her robe unfastening it and letting it fall to the floor.

As if instinctively knowing when she's naked, his eyes avert to her. She lights the candle on the bureau then shuts off the light switch creating an even more beautiful glow in the room. Dane smiles, happy to close his book and put it in the night stand drawer. She watches as he closes the drawer but only after placing something over on her pillow then returning to looking at her with a very pleased smile. She looks from him to her pillow then back at him. He says nothing, reaching his hand behind his head so he can relax and look at her, taking in her goddess like features.

She wants to come to him but she's so curious as to what he put on her pillow and what's got him in such a giving mood. He runs his hand down his chest and onto his stomach. His chest rises and falls beneath mounds of muscle. Her lips smile at how he can arouse her with just breath. He's the most attractive man she's ever seen.

Her eyes wander from his rippled stomach down to the well endowed girth nestled in his sexy underwear. She sees his built thighs and calves and decides she likes this new workout routine he's been doing at the gym in the fire station to work off his stress.

Hazel brings a finger to her mouth wondering if she should just take him anyway she wants or first look at what it is he's placed on her pillow. She stares enjoying the hue of his tan skin in the candlelight, he continues his unhurried breaths, his chest rising and falling as he takes in her nakedness from across the room. He could look at her all night despite her driving him wild. He loves how her hair has grown even longer. Her strands fall along the sides of her breasts and reach down to tickle the smooth skin of her abdomen. She moves her hands to entice him, one along her lower tummy, the other up and cupping under her breast. His eyebrow raises, he loves to see her touch herself but, it always makes him want to join in.

Dane's breath hitches slightly and he feels desire deep within him. She's stoking a fire inside him for the fourth time this week. He can't get enough of her.

Hazel decides that since he placed something on her pillow, she should do the same. He watches her as she steps over to the tall chest-of-drawers and opens the second to the highest drawer reaching on tip toes to find something under her silk panties. He loves sharing an underwear drawer with her and is curious as to what she could searching for from there. She pulls something into her hand and closes the drawer. Turning she stares into his eyes again and places her hands behind her back swaying softly, enticing his curiosity the way he has enticed hers. She tilts her head to the side and smiles in her sexy way. He brings his hands down to the bed and sits up a little higher wondering if he should go to her or stay put for whatever it is she might reveal.

The anticipation is beginning to arouse him in a way that's making him want to get up and take her right up against the wall. He loves how she tempts him with just her eyes. He patiently waits, looking from her pillow back to her sexy bedroom gaze.

Hazel walks gracefully and slow over to her side of the bed and sees what he's been teasing her with. She stops staring down at a tiny black box with a gold band wrapped around it. Startled she looks to him, he smiles wide showing his lovely white teeth and then nods to the box wanting her to open it. He turns his body to the side preparing himself to watch her reaction. She doesn't move, her hands still behind her back as she contemplates giving him the gift she has for him. None of this was planned, it's just another Friday night in, away from the rest of the world. It had been a great week. Her book is taking off, his career is moving forward as he prepares for a rank promotion, life is good, and they are safe inside their own little Melbye world.

Dane's smile moves into a kiss. He offers her one in the air and winks nudging her to open his gift. He raises his hand to offer her guidance onto the bed as he wants her to lie down with him. Hazel shifts her gift to her other hand and uses her free hand to join his. She climbs into bed next to the box, staring at it in disbelief as it looks exactly like what it is and she had no idea he was even thinking of such commitment. But for her, especially *now*, this will work.

Hazel lays her head down next to the box and looks at it, her one hand still behind her back the other tucked under her chin. She loves him more than words can express and is pleasantly surprised by his thoughtfulness. She stares not knowing what to do. She likes their silent communication...and she's *always* liked his body language. Her eyes move her eyes over his body feeling desire to be in his arms again.

He watches her eyes searching them. He loves her eyelashes and the curvature of her facial features. She blinks slow, her eyes moving from him to the black box, then back to his gaze. Her stomach swirls as his sultry gaze still invoke butterflies within her. She wants him, she's never stopped. She inhales and exhales watching him stare back at her. She can play this connection game all night if he wants, although her body yearns for more.

Dane smiles, his lips part but before he says it, he stops and decides to just look at her awhile more. He moves his hand under his cheek and lays along his pillow staring back at the woman he wants forever with...just like this across from him in bed.

Hazel smiles realizing he's waiting for her to speak first. She's decided she's not going to as her question must come after his. He wants to kiss her so badly. Hazel takes her hand and slides it under her cheek copying him. She settles in letting her body language communicate to him that he's in the lead. He returns the smile and takes in a big breath.

"Hazel? Would you?" His eyebrows lift, his eyes sad but eager. He wants nothing more than to make her happy and to be honored to be her husband.

She looks deep into his eyes and decides she'll ask the same but in a slightly different way. Bringing her hand slowly around her body she places her palm down on the sheets between them, her long fingers covering her gift. She looks from her hand to him, back to her hand sliding her palm away and then back to him revealing what she'd been hiding for three months.

Dane Hennie? Would you...marry *us*?"

His eyes focus on the pregnancy test stick for a long moment, his eyebrows furrowing, his face contorts slightly in relief, tears fill his eyes as he lifts them to her, "*Us?*"

Hazel smiles tears falling to her cheeks. She's so honored to have created life with him, "Yes, *us* my hero...both of *us.*"

About the Author

Dezi Golden is an American author of suspense, crime, romance, and other genres. She resides in Las Cruces, New Mexico with her family.